I0689648

RENÉE VIVIEN

A WOMAN APPEARED TO ME

TRANSLATED AND WITH AN INTRODUCTION BY

BRIAN STABLEFORD

THIS IS A SNUGGLY BOOK

Translation and Introduction Copyright © 2019
by Brian Stableford.
All rights reserved.

ISBN: 978-1-64525-001-2

Contents

Introduction

THIS is the third of three volumes translating prose works by Pauline Mary Tarn (1877-1909). The first, *Lilith's Legacy*, contains all the shorter works signed with her best-known pseudonym, originally "R. Vivien" and subsequently "Renée Vivien." The second volume, *Faustina and Other Stories*, contains stories that were originally signed Paule Riversdale—a pseudonym used jointly by Pauline Tarn and Baroness Héléne van Zuylen van Nijevelt van de Haar (née Hélène de Rothschild, 1863-1947)—and some of those that appeared under the French version of the latter signature, but which are believed to be at least partly Tarn's work. This third volume contains the two works entitled *Une Femme m'apparut* that Tarn published as Renée Vivien in February 1904 and August 1905 respectively, which are too dissimilar to be considered merely as a single work that underwent revision between editions.

Une Femme m'apparut is an intensely personal "autobiographical novel," which invites, not to say demands, reading as an account of the author's own feelings and as a kind of confession of her own existential predicament. This certainly does not mean, however, that it is "true" in the trivial sense of representing events that actually happened. The events of Pauline Tarn's life between 1899, when she met Natalie Barney and embarked upon an intense love affair with her, and 1902, when Barney began an intense campaign to resume her relationship after the two had split up and Tarn had begun a new relationship with Hélène de Zuylen, were far more extensive and complicated than those depicted in the "novel," and did not happen in the same order or the same fashion. Biographies of Tarn—the first of which was Jean-Paul Goujon's *Tes Blessures sont plus douces que leurs caresses, vie de Renée Vivien* [Your wounds are sweeter than their caresses; A Biography of Renée Vivien] (1986)—and Natalie Barney's memoirs offer very different accounts of the relationship and its development.

There is, of course, no doubting the sincerity of *Une Femme m'apparut*, but, however scrupulous it is in reproducing the author's feelings at the two points in time when she attempted to summarize and evaluate them, the very attempt to analyze and refine those feelings inevitably attached an exaggerated significance to some events while ruling many others irrelevant and eliminating them from the narrative. Even in physics, as Werner Heisenberg was forced to conclude, the act of observation can alter the properties of what is being observed. That is infinitely truer in the humanities, and acquires a further dimension of complication in literary analysis, which is creative as well as descriptive. "Non-fictional" autobiography is an intrinsically self-serving exercise, essentially a sophisticated species of lying, even when the author strives, in a quasi-sincere fashion, "to lay the heart bare." Quasi-autobiographical fiction, precisely because it is fiction, sometimes allows the author to sidestep some of the intrinsic hypocrisies of "non-fictional" autobiography, but its writing is a far more complex psychological process, in which the component of exploration often outweighs that of explanation, and where the elimination and transfiguration of historical events in the interests of achieving clear and narrower focus routinely produces representations that other observers of the same events could not recognize.

The complexity of that process of transfiguration is especially blatant in the 1904 *Un Femme m'apparut*, in which the author duplicates herself fictionally, featuring in the narrative both as the first person narrator—who never has to be named, simply featuring as "I" and always addressed by the other characters as "you"—and the character named in the text as "San Giovanni," after a famous painting by Leonardo da Vinci, known in Italian as "San Giovanni Battista" and in English as "Saint John the Baptist." The painting, reproduced as a frontispiece in the 1904 version of the text, depicts a face and right arm emerging from darkness, the hand extending a forefinger directed upwards. Were it not for the title, one would probably assume that the figure is female, as the text's San Giovanni is, although she is also referred to sometimes as "the Androgyne." Photographic portraits of Pauline Tarn are scarce, but those that exist certainly license the suspicion that, in looking at that painting in the Louvre, it would have been easy enough to see it as a portrait of herself, representationally as well as symbolically.

That kind of narrative duplication is an exceedingly rare phenomenon, and inevitably creates some confusion for readers attempting to discover the author in the text. There are numerous passages in which the narrator and

San Giovanni are engaged in dialogue, and one crucial passage in which, while separated by distance, they exchange letters. That would not, of course, seem as strange to a writer as it might to a reader, because the process of writing, especially fiction and most especially of all "autobiographical fiction" is often, and perhaps essentially, a kind of dialogue in which the narrative voice engages with the other components of the text. When an author uses fiction as a means of self-exploration, let alone—as is often tacitly the case—as a form of self-therapy, that kind of dialogue is the very heart of the process. Where San Giovanni differs from less obvious fragmentary selves is not so much in her provision of the narrative with an additional alter ego as in the fact that she is so deliberately and teasingly enigmatic. Although she offers advice to her other self relentlessly—including the advice that no one should ever take advice, including hers—most if it turns out to be very dubious in its value.

The distinction between the narrative voice and San Giovanni includes the explicit representation of the former as a writer with abundant citations of her work and several examples of it, whereas the narrative voice claims at one point not to be a writer, although she complains at another point that her distress is spoiling her writing. That distinction is oddly manifest in one of the most peculiar chapters of the 1904 text, when San Giovanni waxes lyrical, at great length, about what a terrible métier that of poet is, and how much she hates it. The text is never fearful of paradoxicality, but it is never pointlessly or flippantly paradoxical, and the bitter complaint that San Giovanni makes against her readers and critics—that they persist in trying to "read the woman" as well as, or instead of, the poetry—can easily be construed as a plea or a challenge addressed to the readers of *Une Femme m'apparut.*

It is, inevitably, a futile plea or challenge. In reading an "autobiographical novel," how can one avoid trying to read the woman as well as the poetry, especially as the whole point of writing the text, from the author's viewpoint, must have been to "read" herself—perhaps, in part, to find herself, and perhaps, in part, to try to heal herself, but certainly to examine and analyze herself? It is worth remembering, however, that *Une Femme m'apparut* was not published bearing the label "an autobiographical novel," and that countless published first-person narratives are anything but autobiographical. Pauline Tarn lived her life secretly, in large measure, and published her fiction under a pseudonym. She had every right to assume that readers approaching the text would have no concept of any mundane reality that might lie, distantly, behind the events and characters of the plot, and would simply read it, as they would read any other novel, as a purely hypothetical account of possible human experience. She knew, however, that most of the critics who were likely to review the book would not—and, indeed, could not—read it in that way, because they already knew, at least vaguely, who "Renée Vivien" was.

It is impossible for anyone likely to acquire this translation not to know that, and it would have done no good to eliminate this introduction, which cannot help but serve as an invitation, if not a demand, to read the woman as well as the poetry. We cannot and need not apologize for that, but it is worth bearing San Giovanni's protests in mind, and sympathizing with her discomfort in experiencing some of the side-effects of the métier of poet. Since she did not take the option of refusing to adopt that métier, however, there is a certain disingenuity in her complaint; conscience ought not to compel readers, therefore, to attempt, impossibly, to see and judge only the poetry and not the woman, but merely to strive to see and judge her as accurately as the text permits.

Significantly, when the author decided to produce a second version of the novel, the character of San Giovanni was marginalized, almost to the point of elimination. Her voice survives in the 1905 version, but it has far less to say directly, and it is very obviously an internal voice speaking from within the consciousness of the narrative voice, distanced from that consciousness solely by way of an evident narrative artifice. As to why the author made that decision, we can only speculate, but it is certainly a dramatic transformation, which would be sufficient on its own to make the second text very different from the first.

In fact, only a third or thereabouts of the 1904 text is reproduced in the 1905 text, where it makes up a little more than half the wordage. The fragments of the 1904 text scattered within the early chapters of the 1905 text are, however, set in different frames in a different order, and are usually modified somewhat. The final chapters of both versions run parallel, and most of the amendments therein consist of a parsimonious abridgment of the text of the 1904 version, but again there are subtle modifications to the preserved text that assist the transformative effects of the abridgment, altering its implications considerably. Whether they improve the poetry or not is a matter of opinion, but the question of whether or not they give a more accurate account of the woman is inevitably confused by the question of how much the woman might have changed between the two versions.

The fact of producing two works under the same title only eighteen months apart is highly unusual in itself, and the author's reason for doing that is not clear. Goujon's biography suggests that she was simply dissatisfied with it, and disappointed by the hostile critical reception that the novel received in some quarters, although he adds the observation that events in the author's life during 1904 had made her considerably less certain of the firmness of her decision to remain with Hélène de Zuylen and resist Natalie Barney's appeals to resume their relationship, increasing her uncertainty as to where her future might lie. He is probably right, and was certainly in a better position to judge than anyone else when he wrote his book in 1986. There are, however, other factors that are worth bearing in mind.

San Giovanni is not the only character who is drastically marginalized in the second version. Some of those eliminated are, in fact, essentially irrelevant to the narrative, and their presence in the 1904 version is gratuitous, but there is one character who functions in the 1904 version as an important narrative lever, represented as the essential cause of the split between the narrator and Vally (the character who stands in for Natalie Barney), who is named there as "the [male] Prostitute." Not only is the character not given that label in the 1905 version, but his presence is so slight and marginal that he no longer qualifies as a narrative lever.

Pauline Tarn could not have been unaware of the fact that in 1903, the Parisian artist Jeanne Jacquemin had sued Jean Lorrain for libel on the basis that he had based a character in an episode of a story series in a leading Paris newspaper on her, and that although the character had a different name, the portrait was clearly recognizable. She was awarded massive punitive damages, which would have bankrupted the author, and set a very ominous precedent had the judgment not fallen on appeal. Tarn must have known while writing *Une Femme m'apparut* that anyone who knew who "René Vivien" was would have no difficult recognizing Natalie Barney as the basis of Vally, but presumably thought that she had nothing to fear from Barney herself, or from any of the other women on whom characters in the novel are based. It might not have occurred to her immediately, however, that the extremely bitter misandry of her portrayal of the male characters might generate some forceful resentments.

One of the characters eliminated in the 1905 version of *Un Femme m'apparut* is Petrus, who is a regular member of Vally's "court"—her salon—tolerated there because of his attractive and talented lesbian wife. The character is clearly recognizable from the description of his person and his circumstances as being based on Joseph Mardus, the husband of Lucie Delarue. The portrait is extremely unflattering, and although it is unlikely to have provoked an explicit threat of legal action, it would not be surprising if Mardus' offended response to it had been communicated to Tarn following publication of the 1904 edition, prompting a diplomatic deletion.

Barney, in her own memoirs, having noted that the first version of *Un Femme m'apparut* had been written while she and the author were not on speaking terms, but that the relationship had been somewhat patched up before the second was written, said : "I had to scold Renée for the first of these 'femmes fatales' who resembled me . . . she declares me 'incapable of loving'—I, who have been capable of nothing else!" and added that: "When I re-read those two novels I get the unpleasant feeling of having posed for a bad portrait artist." The scolding in question seems only to have had a limited effect with respect to her own depiction, in spite of the intervening rapprochement between Tarn and Barney—Lorely, who replaces Vally in the 1905 text, is described at greater length and in greater detail, with more numerous supplementary anecdotes, but is still represented as essentially incapable of love—but Barney's protest might well have increased the author's sensitivity to other possible threats.

The greatest of those possible threats came, undoubtedly, from the individual who provided the basis for the character named as "the Prostitute," easily recognizable by virtue of his engagement to Vally as Barney's one-time fiancé Freddy Manners-Sutton. Perhaps he too would have been extremely reluctant to react to that appellation in court—which would surely have gleaned far more publicity and done far more damage to his image and reputation than the initial libel—but, given the narrator's judgment of his mercenary nature and the Jacquemin/Lorrain precedent, Tarn might not have thought the possibility out of the question once it was pointed out to her.

In view of those circumstances, it is possible that the decision to withdraw the 1904 version of *Une Femme m'apparut* and replace it with a much leaner text, more diplomatic in other respects than in its transfiguration of Natalie Barney, had more reasons than straightforwardly artistic ones—and San Giovanni was no longer present in the second text to protest that such concerns arise from reading the woman rather than the poet. It may be significant that the new characters added to the 1905 text, effectively replacing those deleted from the 1904 text, Doriane and Nedda, are both female, numbered among Lorely's many discarded lovers.

On the other hand, it is also possible that in re-reading the 1904 text herself, Pauline Tarn raised doubts about her own self-portrait. Goujon's biography suggests that Tarn was not nearly as malevolent a misandrist as the narrators of the two texts, and might well have decided, on reflection, that she had gone unnecessarily and unjustly over the top in prose passages presumably written in the heat of the moment. In person, she seems to have been very pleasant, amicable and polite, as many authors are who give a different impression of themselves in print; her supply of bile was, by all accounts, almost exclusively directed inwards. There—to judge by her writings in general, and *Une Femme m'apparut* in particular—it was often transformed into an exaggerated self-disgust that sometimes spilled over while she was writing as a disgust with life, the universe, everything and everyone, with the invariable exception of Psappha and her followers.

Whatever the precise reasons were, however, the 1905 version of *Une Femme m'apparut* is very different, viewed as an ensemble, from its predecessor. It is in some ways a better book, especially seen in purely artistic terms, because rather than in spite of the fact that it seems considerably less revealing and thus less self-injuriously honest, but that does not mean that it can or ought to be regarded as a replacement rather than a supplement. There are, in fact, good artistic grounds for regarding the two texts not as variant versions of a single text but as a greater ensemble, which warrants being read as a whole, and that is the way that they are presented here.

It might seem odd to some readers that I have elected to place the 1905 version ahead of the 1904 version, inviting readers to read them in reverse chronological order. (Anyone who prefers *a priori* not to do that, of course, only has to turn the pages in their own preferred sequence.) It does seem to me, however, that there are good esthetic grounds for reading the leaner, "definitive version" in the first instance, and then adding to its appreciation by seeing, while reading the earlier version, exactly what has been removed and what has been transfigured. That produces, in my opinion, a more satisfactory, more interesting and more revealing experience, not only for those readers, if any, who only want to attend to the poet, but also for those who are interested in the woman.

The poet, of course, is well worthy of attention; as an exercise in Symbolist prose and narrative, *Une Femme m'apparut* is a highly sophisticated and truly exceptional exemplar, offering an unusual combination of delicacy and fervor, economy and flamboyance. Seen purely as a specimen of poetic prose, the 1905 text, in particular, is a masterwork.

Although the spirit of San Giovanni might hold it against me, it also seems to me that the woman is well worthy of attention, all the more so as she is very obviously writing, in this particular interest, about herself and for herself. It is worth observing that Alphonse Lemerre, the publisher of all Tarn's and Zuylen's early works, usually required his authors to pay for the printing of their books, thus speculating against their eventual royalties. While not as rich as Zuylen, Pauline Tarn was sufficiently well off not to be embarrassed by that requirement, and it is certainly not irrelevant to the fact that the two authors published so much so rapidly in 1903-04. While not, strictly speaking, a "vanity publication," it was probably of scant relevance to Tarn whether *Une Femme m'apparut* sold well or not, and she must have expected the hostile critical reception it received, even though it presumably caused her pain anyway.

The hostile reception in question was largely determined by the novel's fervent championship of lesbianism, coupled with its scathing misandry—the coupling is not inevitable, of course—and the novel is certainly extreme in both those respects, but there is far more to the work and to the author than those simple observations. The truly remarkable thing about the psychology of the novel is not the fact that its subject matter is the love of one woman for another but the all-encompassing intensity of the obsession and the agony corollary to it.

If the testimony of the literature of amour can be trusted (and that is a difficult question, by no means rhetorical) then that kind of obsessive, torturing love is something that can easily be experienced by men as well as women, so the fact that Tarn's narrative voice is female ought not to exclude the sympathy of any reader simply on the grounds of her sex or sexuality. If its representation in *Une Femme m'apparut* is truly remarkable—and it is— that has more to do with its complexity, its psychological formation and the manner of its representation than the mere fact of its lesbianism. Nor is it simply a relationship between two individuals—or three, if Eva (the character standing in for Zuylen) is admitted, although she too becomes marginal almost to the point of eclipse in the 1905 version. The third key character in both versions, and the only one whose role is substantially increased as well as significantly transformed in the 1905 text, is Ione (based on Tarn's childhood friend Violette Shillito, who died at a crucial point in the relationship between her and Barney, the spinoff of her death contributing considerably to their break-up).

Even in the 1904 text, the narrator's chaste affection for Ione provides a crucial point of contrast with her painful erotic obsession with Vally, but in the 1905 text Ione, becoming far more distant from her model and suffering far more intensely herself from her own problems, becomes a crucial measuring device against which the narrator judges her own psychology, morality and agony by contrast. The intensity and peculiarity of the narrator's relationship with Ione, and its alteration between the two texts, adds an important dimension to her psychological self-portrait, which has to be given serious weight in any attempt to read the author through the texts.

If due attention is paid to the subject-matter as well as the form and style of the two texts comprising *Une Femme m'apparut*, therefore, it is revealed not only as remarkable but quite unparalleled. There is certainly scope for readers to agree with Natalie Barney's judgment that the texts are direly unfair in the accusations that they level against Vally and Lorely, and to sympathize with her opinion the narrator should simply have stopped whining and learned to love in the lighter fashion of which she was perfectly capable, abandoning her very different, dour and destructive notion of what amour ought to be—but that is not the point. Had Pauline Tarn been able to do that, there would have been no need, and no reason, for her to write the story.

In all probability, the world would be a much nicer place if everyone in despair could simply decide to pull themselves together and be happy instead, but that is not within the bounds of possibility, and while those bounds remain as they are, esthetically expert analyses like the one attempted in *Une Femme m'apparut* remain valuable, enlightening and perhaps even helpful—certainly not as an antidote to despair, but at least as a demonstration that despair has its degrees and its complications, and that no one, however bad they feel, can ever say with certainty that they have the worst of it. Perhaps, in fact, the best thing that can be done in order to counter and resist existential agony and despair is not to seek a "cure" that will restore a "normal" lack of feeling, but instead to channel the pain and despair into art, and thus make it productive. That is what this strange compound work does, with very considerable originality and affective force.

The translation of the 1905 text was made from the London Library's copy of the Lemerre edition, and the translation of the 1904 text from the version reproduced on the Bibliothèque Nationale's *gallica* website. The 1904 text, unusually, has a "musical accompaniment," several bars drawn from sheet music being reproduced at the beginning of each chapter instead of a title. I have not reproduced the musical scores, but I have indicated in each instance the identification of its source, as given in the text.

—Brian Stableford

A WOMAN
APPEARED TO ME

(1905)

Over a white veil circled with olive-trees,
A woman appeared to me, in a green mantle
Clad in the color of bright flame

And my spirit, which for a long time
Had remained such that in her presence
It had not ceased trembling with amazement

Without knowing more via the eyes,
By an occult virtue that came from her,
Felt the great power of ancient amour.
(Dante, *Purgatorio*, Canto XXX.)[1]

---

1 In the continuation of the passage in the *Purgatorio* it transpires that the woman is Beatrice, the once-glimpsed object of Dante's lifelong quasi-erotic obsession. She is now dead, although she is released from Purgatory in order to become the poet's guide in the *Paradiso*—which is, of course, only a dream, Dante always knowing that he is Inferno-bound himself.

I

ON an indecisive evening, the Annunciatrix came toward me.

The face of the Annunciatrix was as mysterious and troubling as that of Leonardo's San Giovanni.

"I pity you," she said to me, "because you have not yet suffered."

I only understood that in part. I was very young.

"I pity your empty heart," she said to me.

Tranquilly, I listened to her.

"I shall take you to Lorely."

"Who is this Lorely?" I spoke with a slight curiosity.

"Lorely is the pagan priestess of a resuscitated cult, the priestess of amour without a husband and without a male lover, as Psappha once was, whom the profane call Sappho. She will teach you the immortal love of female friends."

"Is she beautiful?" I asked.

"Undine[1] herself was not as cruelly and suavely

---

1 The present text renders this name in this form, as in German or English, rather than employing the French Ondine. The capital letter might be taken to imply that the reference is to the character in Friedrich de la Motte Fouque's classic romantic novella *Erzählung* (1811; tr. as *Undine*), but if so the comparison is rather inapt. The 1904 text had rendered the word Ondine, with metaphorical reference to Vally, similarly capitalized.

blonde. Lorely has eyes of icy water and hair the color of moonlight. You will love her and you will suffer from that amour. But you will never regret having loved her."

San Giovanni had said it: I had an empty heart. And I did not yet dread the advent of amour.

"Who knows?" I said to the Annunciatrix. "Perhaps I do not have a heart made for passion. I have not loved. Perhaps I shall not love in my human life. There are so many beings on earth whom amour passes by."

"You will not be one of those, since you will know Lorely."

"Has Lorely loved?"

"I believe that Lorely loves eternal amour more than the ephemeral creatures who incarnate it for her."

I fell silent. The slight curiosity grew within me.

"Will she welcome me favorably, you who know the future?"

"If you love her, Lorely will welcome you, for she likes people to love her. She knows that she is strangely beautiful. She takes pleasure in mirroring her beauty in the fervent eyes of those who adore her."

"When shall I see her?"

"Tomorrow."

The Annuniciatrix smiled at me: an indefinable smile. She smiled like Leonardo's San Giovanni.

II

I waited for Lorely in a glaucous boudoir in which the ornaments seemed to have been thrown here and there by an impatient hand. One sensed the caprice and disorder of an eccentric mind there. There were flowers everywhere, in bunches, sprays and bushy masses. There were tiger lilies opening their vast corollas, which exhaled a violent perfume, clusters of blue orchids dangling with a sad grace, and gardenias, so fragile that the slightest touch would have withered them, paling beside white roses. They were all the flowers of winter, those frail and long flowers that are unable to blossom in the open air and sunlight.

I divined that Lorely must seek in art, rather than in nature, a fugitive ideal.

I began to think . . .

Lorely would appear soon, the incarnation of my destiny. She would come toward me, as cruelly and suavely blonde as Undine herself. San Giovanni observed me with his indefinable smile. I savored that charming anguish of expectation.

The door opened.

"See," said the Annunciatrix.

In a singularly magical half-light, a woman appeared to me. At her approach, the tiger lilies threw off a more vehement perfume.

She was pale and almost supernaturally blonde. Her garments translated the insidious suppleness of her body.

Instinctively, I feared the commandment of her gaze, the imperious curve of her lips. Her hair surrounded her with a perpetual nimbus of moonlight.

I had never seen a stranger beauty.

Lorely dominated me with her gaze. I did not try to escape the seduction of her willful eyes.

"I'm here," I told her, "because I had to come . . ."

She smiled at me, with a Florentine smile that resembled that of the Annunciatrix, but concealed more languor.

"Follow me," she ordered.

She took me by the hand. We entered a luminous studio in which groups of young women were buzzing. They were all beautiful.

Bizarrely gentle, and yet as sharp as two azure flames, Lorely's eyes posed in turn on all those young women; and as they settled on each of them, Lorely's eyes took on a different expression.

"Which of them do you love?" I dared to ask, in a very low voice.

"I love them all," replied Lorely, "but I love each of them with a dissimilar tenderness. Are they not variously beautiful? That one is a living art nouveau painting. How thirsty her lips are for unknown kisses! Her entire being is avid. See, she's as insatiable as a vampire. Her green complexion scorns make-up. One doesn't forget her. Whoever makes contact with her feels it forever . . ."

I admired the slightly green pallor that scorned make-up.

After a pause, Lorely went on ardently:

"Doesn't that one evoke a stray from 1730? Isn't she a Marquise whose feet have retained the memory of minuets? She makes me think of court balls, of powdered wigs, of madrigals whispered behind a fluttering fan . . . That one is a gypsy child intoxicated by sunlight. And over there is a little Gothic virgin. She disdains serene form and line. Look: she seems to have no body beneath her dress with rigid pleats. Simplicity and light are repulsive to her. She only likes the mystical and the miraculous. That other is an Israelite, as magnificent as the Orient, whose hair retains an odor of myrrh and sandalwood . . ."

A very young woman smiled at Lorely.

"Oh, that one . . . that one," murmured the strange beloved, "is the Beauty of dormant desires, the celestial promise . . . I would like to recite a starry sonnet to her. I would like to choose ineffably feminine words for her, to address a worship to her outside the world, to surround her with lilies, incense and candles. I would be the vestal who watches over her sacred body, like an altar. And her blonde candor would only know the subtle lips of charming princesses . . ."

Lorely spoke with a grave tenderness. I divined that that infinite soul could lavish rich emotions, incessantly renewed, without ever exhausting its treasures.

"And me," I implored, "and me, Lorely, will you not love me?"

Lorely considered me, anxiously.

"I believe that I will love you," she said. "I believe that I love you already . . ."

The daylight was declining, and the dusk mingled its tender mystery with those mysterious and tender words.

"Expect me this evening," I whispered. "I'm avid for stars . . ."

III

WE left together. We wandered in a wood frosted by the winter evening. Like a Scandinavian princess, Lorely was enveloped in white furs.

My eyes were dazzled by the snow. All that light seemed florid with unreal espousals.

Lorely fell silent.

"Talk to me about yourself," I begged. "I love you, and I would like to be a little less ignorant about the woman I love."

"I'm sad, without any veritable distress," Lorely replied. "I'm indescribably sad . . ."

"Are you not in love with sadness?"

"No. I flee it, and yet I always find it in everything. I lament in vain, like the autumn wind . . ."

She stopped.

"My life distresses me," she continued, "but I can't imagine a better life. The luxury that surrounds me oppresses me. The pleasures are so old that their bite is toothless."

"From what sickness are you suffering in your soul?"

"From what sickness?" Lorely sighed. "I don't know. Whatever it is, I'm incurable. My heart is a bell with a cracked timbre . . ."

10

She laughed, bitterly.

An anguish gripped my heart. I loved her already . . . I loved her already . . .

"Ennui! It seems to me, sometimes, that the universe is like a gray cathedral, from which Our Lady of Old Age has banished the gods. She alone reigns, the wrinkled Madonna, in her crumbling reliquary . . ."

She went on:

"Sometimes, I tell myself that I have sung all my songs and picked all my flowers. But I sense that my soul remains thirsty. I'm still waiting for I know not what. I still sigh, but I don't know for what. Perhaps it's a new amour, an unknown amour, for which I hope. Perhaps you'll bring me that amour, in your extended hands . . ."

Around us was the winter evening, an evening of mystical marriage. Around us and within us there was a nuptial chastity, a white sensuality.

"I would like so much to love you!" sighed Lorely.

Those words fell upon my troubled heart.

"I know that I love you, Lorely . . ."

An obscure prescience dictated these words to me: "I love you and I already have the certainty that you will never love me. However, I'm not afraid of loving you. You are the marvelous suffering that makes one scorn happiness."

I added, when Lorely remained silent: "I saw you today for the first time, and already I'm the shadow of your shadow. I shall be what you make of me."

"I love your love," murmured Lorely. "I'm afraid of understanding you, and I hesitate to attract you irremediably. My illusions are poor clowns that look at one another grimacing through their tears. I would like so much to love you, to love you in my moments of silence, which would finally be eternalized. Do you not see how I weep at my joy and laugh at my sadness?"

There was a pause between us.

"My amour is great enough to remain solitary," I replied. "I love you, and that is sufficient for my ecstasy and my sobs. You will never love me, Lorely, for you have within you such an ardor to live, and to feel, that the passion of all beings could never content you . . ."

The stars were shining as coldly as the frost. And beneath our feet the snow was luxuriously unrolled.

Lorely's hair was scintillating coldly with a lunar radiance. And Lorely's eyes were coldly blue, like water bathed by moonlight.

"I'm drunk," I sobbed. "Lorely, I'm drunk . . ."

Around us there was the winter evening, the evening of unreal espousals . . .

IV

I submitted to a strange felicity, without understanding it and without savoring it. Only later did I know that those troubled hours were the unforgettable hours that weep regrets and memories.

"Lorely will teach you the immortal amour of female friends," the Annunciatrix had murmured.

Lorely was like a pagan priestess who, in an abandoned temple, had resuscitated the worship of the goddess, re-ignited the sacred fires and rebuilt the ruined altar. She spoke about Psappha as if she had heard her sing in an orchard in Mytilene. None of the companions of the weaver of violets had ever loved her more simply or more fervently than that distant disciple.

"She alone," said Lorely, "is eternal. The cult of the gods has perished, but the cult of her poems will never perish. Whoever loves her must love her to the exclusion of any other amour."

And I remembered noble words dedicated to Psappha, gleaned from a book, which I had often reread:

> *If you love me, you will quit everything that*
> *you cherish, and the places that you remember*
> *and those for which you hoped, and your mem-*

ories and your hopes will no longer be anything but desire for me.

If you love me, you will not look either backwards or forwards, you will only know me, and your destiny will go no further than my imprint.

If you love me, you will have no other infinities than my lips, no other prisons than my arms, and of my body you will make all your dreams . . .

And I replied to her, sobbing: "I love you."[1]

---

1 Author's reference: "Tryphé, *Cinq petits dialogues grecs*. Paris, La Plume." As a trivial noun, the Greek *tryphé* referred to a kind of luxurious and libidinous self-indulgence, similar to one of the meanings subsequently attached to the term "decadence." As a proper noun Natalie Barney used it as a pseudonym for her publication of the book in question in 1902.

V

I loved Lorely with all the unconscious impetus of my first amour. I loved her so blindly that I did not ask myself whether that love was shared. I loved Lorely, and I still believed that love attracts love.

Gradually, I awoke, and I understood that Lorely remained indifferent to all my passion, to all my tenderness.

Time, far from bending her, fixed her in her coldness. My footsteps, my voice and my presence irritated her. She did not love me, and never would love me, ever.

When, stupidly, I lamented over that for which neither of us was responsible, she replied:

"It's me who ought to lament and you that it's necessary to envy. Since you've been able to discover the amour for which I've been searching in vain for so many wasted years, reveal it to me. I would like so much to love you."

And when I implored her for a word of hope, she said again: "I would like so much to love you," like a refrain of her lips, weary of mine.

Sometimes, she let me glimpse the possibility of attaining it one day.

"Later, you will understand the negligibility of the pleasures for which I neglect you. And you will only see then, in the avidity with which I seek them, my fear of seeing them vanish."

She had for symbols the rainbow and the opal, everything that shines and changes in accordance with a momentary reflection.

"Like art," she said, "Amour is complex and troublesome. The sculptor does not seek his superhuman vision in a single model. He discovers absolute splendor in dissimilar beings, each of whom has given him what each had of the most beautiful. And for my dream of amour, it is necessary for me to combine scattered perfections, in order to confound them in a harmonious whole created by me."

One day, I said to her:

"You are April. Only these lines by Swinburne can express and contain you entirely: 'A mind of many colors, and a mouth/of many tunes and kisses . . .'[1] But for myself, I love you dolorously and with a unique amour."

"You love me badly," interrupted my flower of Selene. "You love me badly, since you are unable to retain me or to comprehend me."

"One always loves badly, Lorely. To love well is no longer to love amorously."

"Amour?" Lorely repeated. "Amour is perpetual self-immolation. When I encounter in passing an apparition of grace that delights me, you ought to rejoice in the felicity granted to me by a brief illusion."

She quoted: "I have dreamed of a Calvary where roses flourish . . ."[2]

"Perhaps you have the better part," I conceded.

And we united our feverish lips in a kiss in which we could already taste the bitterness of future regrets.

---

1 The lines are from "Anactoria." The verse continues: "And she bowed,/With all her subtle face laughing aloud,/Bowed down upon me, saying: 'Who doth thee wrong,/Sappho?'"
2 The quotation is from a poem in Natalie Barney's *Quelque portraits: sonnets de femmes* (1900).

VI

WHO could ever describe the varying, ungraspable charm of Lorely?

Often, we wandered together in the little wood, similar to enchanted forests. A mysterious silence reigned there. One could have believed oneself amid the verdure of Broceliande, where Viviane once roamed.

Viviane! I evoked the fay temptress, representing her under the appearance of Lorely. Viviane's eyes were a mortal blue. Her wavy hair paled like moonlight. She smiled, like Lorely, thinly. With a perfidious slowness she slid through the creepers, collecting hemlock and foxgloves in passing. And her kiss gave forgetfulness.

Lorely was a distant sister of Viviane.

The fallacious spring had come, lavishing its deceitful promises, giving birth to the thirst for impossible happiness.

Like all souls, I listened to the promises of spring, and my gaze turned toward Lorely, who incarnated the deceptive April fully.

"It seems to me," Lorely whispered, "that this spring will finally bring me the unknown sweetness for which I've always hoped. It seems to me that I too am going to be reborn, that I shall warm up, that I shall blossom entirely. Do you hear? I sense that tomorrow, I shall love truly. Perhaps it's you that I shall love . . ."

She dazzled me with a smile.

Spring surrounded Lorely like a stage-set. I had never seen her more radiant. She went forth, chimerically supple, and one would have thought that she was marching toward the future.

"Tomorrow," she said, "oh, tomorrow, I shall love . . ."

Along the edge of the little wood, an idle stream snaked. We went along the path that led to that stream.

On the edge, where the reeds were quivering, Lorely stopped.

"Come and lean over the water," she said.

She knelt down and looked at her reflection. I reached for nenuphars, which she mingled with her unfastened hair, laughing.

"You're more beautiful than Undine," I sighed.

I held out my arms to her. I wanted to imprison her in my embrace. She would be mine . . . finally mine. Her heart would respond to my heart. Her eyes would respond to my ardent eyes. Perhaps she would abandon herself, consenting . . .

But she slipped out of my hands and stole away, like a fugitive undine . . .

And, sad in my impossible desire, I considered her.

Her green dress flowed around her fluid body. The glaucous pleats undulated in the sun. She seemed clad in eddies . . .

"Will you escape me eternally, Lorely?"

"Perhaps so . . ."

The indecisive words streamed in the silence. Sobs rose from my throat.

"Don't cry," she ordered. "Think of the ugliness of tears."

She broke a reed and put it between my fingers.

"Here's a flute," she said. "Make it sing to me, since you love me . . ."

I took the reed. I tried to sculpt it, to animate it with my breath. Wasted effort: the reed remained mute. I had to confess my defeat.

"I can't make it sing for you, Lorely."

She pouted, with a delightful chagrin.

"How can I love you, since you can't make it sing for me?"

She went back into the little magic wood. The sun vivified her pale hair and her feet sparkled in the grass. An invisible orchestra seemed to accompany her, translating her, expressing her very quietly.

I followed her, my soul discouraged. She paused, leaning back against an oak. She stood against the tree for a long time, its foliage raining down around her. Knowing that she needed silence, I did not say anything.

"I can hear the heart of the tree beating," she murmured, "and the green blood flowing in its veins."

The foliage famed her with moving reflections, and the slightly glaucous blondes of her hair were impregnated with emerald. She evoked and resuscitated the slender grace of a Hamadryad.

I contemplated her. And I understood the insatiable amour of woman that drives peoples to seek it everywhere, in springs and rivers, in the forest and the sea: Hestia, springing from vivid flame; Pomona, rounding out the soft curve of fruits; Flora; kneaded from all perfumes;

Maenads, who were the tumultuous souls of vines; Naiads and Nereids . . . the universal Good Goddess!

I rediscovered in Lorely the fugitive naiad, the nereid, the oread with the calm hair, the maenad and the vestal. And above all, I rediscovered in her the harmonious peril that the sirens symbolized . . .

I only saw her, and I only pursued her image in the multiple magnificence of the universe. I worshiped, in the beauty of Lorely, the immortal beauty of woman . . .

She understood what I was thinking.

"You're right; I'm eternal. I shall die, but I shall be reborn, and those who love my memory will always recognize me."

And, her eyes shining with pride, she said: "I shall be resuscitated tomorrow, as I am resuscitated today . . ."

VII

I went out in the crepuscular rain, and intoxicated myself mortally with the marvelous sadness of evening drizzle. I bore a feverish melancholy in my heart.

"Lorely . . ." I murmured through the drizzle. "Lorely . . ."

Her name returned to my lips like a sob.

I evoked the already distant hour when I saw her for the first time, and the frisson that ran through me when my eyes met hers. I had had a premonition that that woman incarnated my destiny, that her face was the redoubtable face of my future.

With her I had known the luminous vertigos that rise from the abyss and the appeal of exceedingly deep water.

I had not attempted to flee, for it would have been easier for me to escape death.

As I thought about those things, I perceived a crepuscular form coming toward me, that one might have thought woven out of the declining light and the rain. Gradually, that form drew closer and became more precise. I recognized Ione.

Ione had been the little companion of my childhood. We had grown up side by side, putting all our thoughts in common. She had remained the pure sisterly soul. But I had not yet dared to mention her to Lorely.

My eyes attached themselves to Ione. The overly broad and high forehead overwhelmed the whole of that pensive face, hypnotizing gazes and almost causing the vast eyes, as brown as the evening, and the tender mouth to be forgotten.

Like a nun, Ione walked with her eyes lowered. A perfume of solitude floated around her. Her voice and her gestures had a religious softness.

She was carrying dolorous violets between her fingers. She loved violets among all flowers, for their grave simplicity.

"Ione," I said to the melancholy friend, "give me your sadness. I'll add it to mine."

She smiled, without replying.

"You seem to be wandering through this evening drizzle in search of a shelter," I went on, forcing myself to be flippant.

"You're not mistaken. I'm searching desperately for a shelter."

I was slightly astonished by the impetuous solemnity of that response. We exchanged a long gaze.

"I'm tired of searching," she added. Her voice translated an unfathomable discouragement.

"I'm going to repose in a chapel not far from here. There are neither hymns nor the sound of the organ at this hour, only pious silence. The little flames of candles puncture the shadow and the gold of the altars gleam faintly. One divines the pensive Madonna and the tragic Christ. The evening has drowned their faces and the breath of lilies rises toward them. The odor of incense is a pacifying intoxication."

"Ione," I begged, "don't stay too long in the chapel . . ."

She was not listening to me.

"I kneel down at the feet of the pensive Madonna, the Madonna who welcomes all prayers, and I put mine in her hands. In all chapels, there's always a woman weeping at the feet of the Madonna. I'm that woman. I don't hear the people who go by and brush past me. I remain sunk in my sadness and my hope."

"What hope, Ione?"

She hesitated.

"It seems to me then . . . it seems to me, in truth, that I believe . . ."

"How can you believe, Ione, in confrontation with the suffering of beings?"

Her lips parted hesitantly, and then she went on:

"I interrogate the mute Virgin who gives the impression of taking pity on me too. I have my share of her universal compassion. The incense rises toward her, carrying my soul away. I'm kneeling down, lost in the dusk—one little shadow amid all that shadow. I feel humble and infinitely tender. In sum, I'm no longer thinking . . ."

"Yes, yes, don't think any more, my dear love. Love someone, love something. Amour is less deadly than thought."

Ione drew away slightly.

"I've never loved and never will love a human being, who would be as feeble and lamentable as me. What I desire, recklessly, is the divine. I want a love that will never be deceived or disappointed, an endless and limitless love, a supernatural love. I want faith."

Ione's face paled in the dusk. She stared at her hands, the color of old ivory. She had an unhealthy habit of contemplating her hands for hours.

A veiled woman went past us. She continued on her way, groping.

"She's going to the chapel," said Ione. "She's going to pray. Perhaps she believes . . ."

The gripping word of a blind man heard in Tunis returned to my memory:

Give me a little money, in order to buy light.

In a loud voice, I completed my thought. "We all forget that light isn't for sale. We're the blind. And we exhaust our will uselessly in the effort to see, instead of closing our eyes and looking into ourselves. The light is inside us, not outside. We'll only see it when we resign ourselves to not seeing anything."

Ione's eyes were following the woman, already distant, who gradually disappeared into the mist.

"Perhaps she believes . . ."

"And you, Ione, don't you believe?"

With a heavy regret, she shook her head.

"I haven't yet been invited to the festival of the miracle . . ."

I shivered.

"Those who believe conceal within them all the magnificence of the heavens," Ione said. "What does it matter if they're mistaken? They've known Paradise. They've entered into it alive . . ."

She repressed her tears. I remained before her, impotent to soothe her or to cure her.

"You know my entire life," she went on. "Do you remember my distress when, on emerging from childhood, I lost my faith? I've never consoled myself for having lost it. Sometimes, it seems to me that I'm going to die of no longer believing."

She drew closer to me. Her entire being was in revolt

against the horror of the real, against the ugliness and the baseness of the real.

The twilight enveloped us, as gray and bleak as doubt, and the indecision of the hour was full of anguish. Unquiet light vacillated on the horizon.

"Nothing is assured," said Ione, in a voice that broke. "See, the universe is as uncertain as our souls."

Around us, the twilight became sadder, like doubt.

"Our poor souls . . . ," sighed Ione.

An exclamation escaped me. "Ione . . . Ione . . ."

"Come," my friend commanded. "We'll repose in the chapel, since it's the hour of silent prayer."

She hastened, as a sick person hastens toward a spring of miraculous cures. I followed her as far as the threshold of the chapel, the door of which was ajar.

In the depths of the shadow rose a Virgin with joined hands. Her crown of stars cast glimmers, and her feet rested on a submissive moon.

"Come," said Ione, again.

I hesitated on the threshold of the sanctuary. And the image of Lorely was interposed . . .

She was shining with all her perverse whiteness. Her morbid hair spread out, moonlight in the dusk. Her eyes, of an Apriline blue, a suave and deceptive blue, drew me, appealed to me. She murmured, very quietly:

"Perhaps I shall love you, later . . ."

And it was Lorely who reigned above the altar. Over her unfastened hair shone a crown of stars. Her bare feet trampled the submissive moon . . .

Alongside Ione, I went into the sanctuary. The lilies exhaled their sacred perfumes toward Lorely and the candles dedicated their flames to her.

I knelt down before Lorely's altar and I offered to Lorely the most fervent, the most reckless, of orisons . . .

VIII

LIKE every nostalgic soul, Lorely sought with complaisance the prestige of strange garments, which travesty minds as well as bodies, and resuscitate, for an hour, the grace of a vanished epoch.

Sometimes, she put on the costume of a Venetian page, a lunar green velvet costume that harmonized with her hair. Her fingers wandered over a lute. She had the feverish slenderness of an amorous child and her gestures took on something simultaneously willful and suppliant.

"I'm a page infatuated with the Dogaress," Lorely said. "She's so arrogantly beautiful, in her gondola, whose prow in encrusted with gold and emeralds. I carry her train, and from time to time she lets a distracted glance fall upon me; and I would die if she neglected to cast that insouciant glance at me . . ."

Sometimes she transformed herself into a little Greek shepherd. The music of an invisible syrinx then rose up around her footfalls, and her eyes laughed at the nudity of faunesses. Sometimes, too, she was a tall and sad chatelaine, whose robe maintained very chaste pleats inflexibly. She sat down in a pose of dejection, on a seat as narrow as a church stall, and, as if she were talking in her solitude, she murmured languid words very quietly.

"I'm bored . . . I'm so bored that I sometimes surprise myself regretting my husband's absence. Will I weep if he's killed out there in the Holy Land? I don't believe so. But here, I'm dying of boredom. I'm weary of contemplating, by turns, the flight of the clouds and the illuminations of my missal. I'm weary of imagining innumerable sins, in order to confess them to the good monks, whose naïve embarrassment I enjoy. My page is a foolish child with shiny red cheeks. I could recite the stories that my four maidservants recount to me too frequently all the way through. In any case, they're stupidly ingenuous. In truth, I'm mortally bored . . ."

Lorely was, by turns, a Byzantine princess, a young English lord whose slim build and fine clothes François I might have noticed in the Field of the Cloth of Gold, an unhealthy and cruel infanta, a wandering minstrel without any other wealth than his harp. Sometimes, she was an Egyptian dancer, sometimes she was a fay clad in iris petals, wearing gems of sparkling dew.

She was different, while retaining her indefinable charm.

"I'm striving to escape from myself," she said, adjusting her adornments of another age and a distant land. "That's how I console myself miserably for not having been able to forget myself completely, to transform myself by the magic of a veritable amour."

Feverishly, she chose and rejected fabrics and jewelry.

"I'm always similar to myself," she sighed.

And that long sigh was tragic, like a lamentation.

Lorely had an instinctive worship of the artificial. She loved to powder her pallor with pink. The false redness of her cheeks then contrasted in a disconcerting fashion with the attenuated light of her hair.

"To get as far away as possible from nature; that's the true goal of art," she said. "The artist who strives to imitate nature is only a vulgar copyist. Only the creator is indisputably an artist. In painting, I only like psychic landscapes, flowers of dream and faces that one will never contemplate."

Like Aphrodita, Lorely possessed a thousand souls and a thousand appearances. And I loved her through all of her metamorphoses.

Those who cherished her suffered from seeing her distracted in their arms and always unsated. Some wept, others charged her with reproaches. A few others remained riveted to her by their very suffering. Yet others had understood that Lorely's heart was heavy with melancholy, with an intolerable need to love.

She would have given her youth, her beauty and her complex intelligence to experience the naïve sobs of a sincere passion, to love like the simplest women. And that unappeased thirst rendered her, at intervals, impatient and grim. One might have thought that she bore a grudge against her lovers, and against me, for the amour that we could not make her feel.

IX

YOUNG WOMEN and girls crowded around Lorely, in quest of her fleeting smiles and caresses.

"I want them," she sobbed through her clenched teeth. "I desire them implacably."

And her eyes were sharp then, like a blue steel blade.

"I love what they have of the fugitive, of the ungraspable, everything that I shall never possess of them. And the incomplete sensuality that I drink from their mouths is more precious than happiness, prosaic material happiness . . ."

She added, in a lower voice: "And yet . . . and yet . . . oh, if I were able to love!"

She did not love the passers-by that stole her from me. However, I envied them, for they had had from her, if only for an instant, an amorous kiss.

X

"So you're going to marry!"

Lorely's voice had become mordant and somber.

The person who was listening to her shivered slightly. She was a child with the profile and the twitter of a bird, who gave an impression of aerial weakness.

Lorely went on with intensity: "You're going to immolate your limpid twenty years in your turn!"

She fell silent, as if to collect herself in her bitterness and her anger.

"You're going to consecrate your love before the church, whose ready-made formulae and obligatory oaths you'll accept. And thus you'll impose slavery on your future children in advance. You don't understand how humiliating and immoral legitimate union is. And above all, above all, you're accepting today that you'll submit tomorrow to vile male lust."

The child blushed to the roots of her hair, chestnut striped with gold.

"You'll be a wife and a mother—later, no doubt, bourgeois!" the bitter Lorely continued.

She had stood up like an avenging angel.

"And you'll give to the future another moan, another suffering. Have you never heard the plaint of the entire human race? Have you never thought about the horror of living and the horror of dying? Those two tortures you're going to inflict, without dread and without remorse, on your impotent posterity . . ."

A religious terror chilled Lorely's wrath. She spoke with a profound apprehension.

"You're going to animate nothingness. You're going to make non-being live. And what destiny is reserved for those creatures of tomorrow? Anguish, malady, old age and death. Have you not reflected that one day, your daughters and your sons will curse you for having created them, for having throwing them as fodder to fatal dolor?"

The child's gaze wandered. Hesitantly, she replied: "All the world isn't miserable and sad."

But Lorely, drawing nearer to her, seized her wrists, as if to impose her fervent conviction upon her. Her breath burned the young woman's forehead. All her strength was concentrated in the unique determination to dominate that soul.

"The happy? Where are they? And if there are any on the face of the globe, of what monstrous egotism is their happiness made?"

Tears rose to the adolescent's eyes. Lorely was still holding her.

"You haven't understood me. You haven't known me. I've offered you both passion and tenderness. Above all, I've brought you beauty. Perhaps I would have made you suffer. But you'd have wept such beautiful tears!"

She went on:

"I've brought you, myself, the dream, in my hands hollowed out in the fashion of cups. The man you're marrying can only offer you realities—and what hideous, what sordid realities! But you prefer the reality to the dream . . ."

Lorely let go of the frail wrists that her feverish fingers were bruising.

"Go to your destiny. You've wanted mediocrity and ugliness. You've summoned marriage and maternity. So be it. Don't turn round, don't look back; you'd see me weeping, and I don't permit anyone to surprise my tears . . ."

The imperious voice had broken.

"Later, oh, later, I'll remember you with a lamentable tenderness. I'll bury you, like a corpse, in the utmost depths of my memory, and I'll throw the flowers of my folly over your memory. Time will change into regret what remains in me of love for you . . ."

The child bowed her head.

"Promise of heaven," murmured Lorely, "promise of heaven, how you've unknowingly deceived me!"

She sighed.

"Another passer-by in whom I thought I recognized the one for whom I'm searching! One more rancor added to the others, one more disillusionment; and the fear of seeing, trailing in their wake, indifference and the inevitable ennui. Will my heart be dried out one day by lassitude and disgust?"

Then, resuming:

"I'll evoke you so cruelly when the heavy season of harvests comes! How I hate it, that moment when all amour bears its fruit! The foliage no longer has its freshness, nor the flowers their virginity. The earth has settled down, and fecundity prevails over amour. Nothing is vibrant or chaste any longer; the universe is sated with kisses and grapes. Then . . . then I'll search in vain within me for the image of your sacrificed spring."

With a sovereign gesture, she drew the young woman toward her and gave her a kiss of adieu.

"I might have been able to love you," Lorely whispered.

She closed her eyes, and said to the trembling child:

"Soon, weary of containing my pain, I shall weep . . . I shall weep through my poorly closed eyelids. Oh, the harm that my eyes do me! Oh, the harm that remains to me for having contemplated you, for having seen you so dissimilar to yourself, for having felt . . . Blind me, kill my eyes . . . through my eyes, as if through two wounds, I sense you . . . and I'm suffering . . ."

But a surge of energy brought her upright again.

"In spite of all your coldness, I shall burn you. One day, you'll understand my gaze, and you'll know . . . You'll be afraid . . . And you'll give yourself to me as to your dreams . . . Oh, beloved, I'll be gentle and I'll be similar to you, held by the same desire, the same thought, yours beyond all the words that separate us . . ."

Discouragement gripped her, and she murmured:

"The lassitude of loving is death. And that death is gradually gaining me. Tomorrow—who knows?—I might talk about love without shivering and without remembering. I'll be similar to an old woman, still young, who will have forgotten, by virtue of no longer living—or living differently—her youth. I'll be weary of loving, I'll be dead . . ."

The little virgin knotted her arms round Lorely's neck and promised, in a breath:

"I'll break off my engagement. I don't love him, that rude man. I only love you . . ."

Violently, Lorely drew her toward her. Her voice sang, victoriously:

"An elemental joy like that of the tides draws me toward you, carries me toward our happiness. Oh, I sense that I can finally love, that I love you . . . yes, that I love you . . ."

XI

THE little virgin broke off her engagement, as she had promised the beloved. A few weeks later, Lorely wearied of her, and the child wept for two happinesses destroyed.

XII

AMONG all her jewels, Lorely preferred a necklace of moonstones.

"I'm adorned with the moon's tears," she said, smiling.

One evening, I found her strangely joyful. Her hair was unfastened and sown with tobacco flowers. Over her gray velvet dress, opaque moonlight, her necklace of tears glittered coldly.

She laughed on seeing me: musical and broken laughter.

"I don't recognize you," I said. "You're beautiful, in a different manner."

"I am, in fact, different," Lorely threw at me. "You don't know my nocturnal soul yet. I can't be myself as long as the daylight lasts, but by night, my personality is exasperated and refined. I'm fully myself, in my wisdom and my folly. I told you once that what seems to me to be unreasonable by day becomes logical with the approach of darkness. By night, everything is extraordinary, and the most mediocre human beings can live their moment of the unreal. Come . . ."

I had never seen her as desirable. The suspended lighting revealed all her dream-like grace, made to be contemplated by the light of the moon and the stars.

"The night is ours," said Lorely. "To others the day. Follow me. You'll see the colors of the night, you'll hear its songs, and you'll respire its odors. Let's go to the forest, where the lake in which Undine reflects herself scintillates amid the trees like a fallen mirror. You'll see how bright it is amid the shadows."

She meditated.

"Or rather," she continued, "let's go into the marshes where the fire follets wander."

"The marshes are perilous," I objected.

But Lorely laughed louder.

"As long as the darkness lasts, folly is the greatest wisdom."

She bounded forward. Her dress had mysterious frissons of nocturnal wings. I followed her to the marshes.

Fire follets were running in the night.

"How beautiful they are!" Lorely ecstasized. "How strangely beautiful they are!"

"They're spectral torches," I said, shivering.

"No, they're the candles of amorous festivals."

Quivering, Lorely launched herself in pursuit of them.

"Lorely," I implored, "slow down. The route is uncertain and the dormant marshes perfidious."

She fled without hearing me. She resembled a stray ray of moonlight.

She bounded toward the illusory fire follets.

"Oh, to collect them and carry them away in my hands!"

Lorely fled, like a shooting star at sky level. Soon, she was no more than a silvery dot in the marshes. And with sweat on my temples and anguish in my heart, I ran without being able to catch up with her. She was ungraspable. I exhausted my strength, my will and my courage vainly pursuing a fire follet more beautiful than the rest . . .

XIII

LORELY'S sensuality was infinitely pure, her desire infinitely chaste. "I can't," she said, "trace the limits of my body or my soul, my body having a soul and my soul a body."

Lorely confirmed herself with a singular frankness. She emphasized her individuality as few individuals have the audacity to do, unaware of little lies and affirming that, in her full personality, she was above rules and laws.

She seemed to have gone astray in our epoch. She was an exile from Mytilene, bearing eyes full of memories of that unknown world. Her pagan soul searched, regretfully, for the harmonious homeland. At all times, she was outside the present hour.

One day before Christmas she asked me: "What is this Festival of Noel? Does it commemorate the birth or death of Christ? I can no longer remember."

Perhaps she had never known . . .

XIV

THE east wind blew over the denuded space. At a bend in the road I encountered the most beautiful of Lorely's friends.

Doriane was as brown as Psappha herself. Her dark eyes had the color of Oriental darkness, and her slenderness concealed a singular vehemence and strength. She was habitually withdrawn, like a wild animal in repose.

Lorely's smile had revealed its regal indifference to her. And Lorely had loved her for a time for the magnificence of her passion, which expressed itself in incomparable speech and letters.

But gradually, Lorely had detached herself from her, because, eloquent as her tenderness was, it was not the Impossible.

Doriane had been obstinate in the conquest of that soul. She hung on, with a tenacious despair, to the amour that was slipping away.

I had a moment of amazement on perceiving her. Her fixed gaze only contained one unique thought. One sensed that her entire being was extended in the continuity of that effort.

She came straight to the point.

"You love Lorely," she said to me. "I sense that you understand me. Lorely doesn't love me."

I dared not abuse her with false affirmations. One owes sincerity to great dolors.

Doriane read my thoughts, for she added: "I'm suffering, therefore I have the right to absolute truth. She alone can help me. It's necessary not to refuse me."

"I won't deceive you," I promised. "I'll even help you if I can. I suffer even more from seeing Lorely wander, her heart empty, than I'd suffer from knowing that she was distanced from me irredeemably by a veritable amour."

Doriane listened to me, very pale. "I want her to love me," she hissed, between clenched teeth.

My gesture of discouragement replied to her. "Nothing will ever fill her heart."

"But amour can do anything," Doran interjected. "It's persuasion and constraint combined. It's irresistible."

I smiled sadly.

"I'll force her to love me," Doriane continued. "I'll surprise her, I'll violate her soul. I'll impose my sobs and my dreams upon her. She won't escape me. I'll transform myself in order to please her. I'll be indescribably patient. I'll learn all the ruses. I'll divine what her gaze hides; I'll be untiring in spying on her, in following her. She'll love me in spite of herself, because I love her."

"May you be loved by Lorely, Doriane! There will be so much joy in my dolor when she says to me: 'I love in accordance with my dream . . .'"

"I don't understand you," said Doriane, impetuously. "It was necessary to make yourself loved; it's necessary to struggle with more energy, as I shall struggle, without ever admitting defeat."

"Once, I hoped and I was obstinate . . . Perhaps you will also know one day the poignant pride of loving without being loved. There's a melancholy pride in saying to oneself: 'My love is great enough not to demand anything not to want anything. It is nourished by its own substance, and bears its tenebrous joy within itself . . .'"

Doriane shook her beautiful head vehemently. She repeated: "She will love me, since I love her with such a willful amour!"

And I said to her: "May you not fail, Doirane."

"I'm going to see her," she threw at me.

She drew away.

I stayed in the same place. Suddenly, I heard a sound of parted branches. Lorely was in front of me, laughing.

"You look bewildered. Nothing is as stupid as astonishment. It's necessary never to be surprised by what I do. With me, anything is possible; whimsy is my rule, and only the bizarre and the unexpected are natural to me."

"So you heard everything that Doriane and I said?"

"Enough to assure myself that your conversation didn't interest me."

"Why don't you love her, Lorely? She's passionate and beautiful."

"Perhaps I'd love her if she didn't love me at all. After all, what do I know? Perhaps I'll love her later. But today, I'm not in a humor to love anyone. I feel as free as the wind. Oh, how I admire the wind for being strong and immense."

We were standing at the intersection of four roads, which all ended in a savage plain. The grass had been browned there by the summer fires that Bohemians light, and the wind was blowing incessantly over the denuded soil.

Her face raised toward the sky, and her hair unfastened, Lorely suddenly shouted: "Look at the flight of the hectic clouds!"

The entire sky was nothing but a crazy disordered racecourse.

"Can't you see the wind itself running beneath the clouds?" Lorely panted. "It has no wings; what would it do with them? It would weary all wings. It has long, floating hair, a woman's hair, and a woman's dress with tumultuous pleats. A beautiful thing, to see the wind racing!"

She let herself fall on to the gray grass.

"Today, I sense, more than I've ever sensed it before, eternal mobility," she said, excitedly. "How dare you talk to me about love before that great haste of things toward the unknown?"

And, bounding to her feet: "I'm going to strive to run as fast as the wind itself . . ."

Lorely fled, like the wind, the clouds and the earth, and I fled too. The universe drew us along in its vertiginous race, and nothing any longer remained either fixed or durable. There was no longer anything but our great haste toward the unknown . . .

XV

I sometimes went to visit the silent Ione. I always found her clad in an ample dark red dress that, I don't know why, put me in mind of evenings in Florence. Ione liked wearing a ruby belt and a pendant of hieratic design composed of a ruby mounted in green gold and terminated by a baroque pearl.

I spent taciturn hours with Ione. I dared not talk to her about Lorely. I wasn't apprehensive of the censure of that soul, whose purity was ennobled by a very broad comprehension, but I sensed that Ione's tenderness would be alarmed by my tortures, divined in spite of my reticence. She knew, like me and better than me, how sterile my impossible effort to conquer the indifferent heart of Lorely—who did not love me and never would love me—would be. She was not unaware that I was exhausting myself in futile suffering. And that thought darkened further the sadness of her eyes, as ardently brown as an autumnal night.

The constraint that weighed upon our words determined a distancing of souls between us. We feared one another's gaze as one fears a confession, and we feared our silences as treasons. We were afraid of the truth, and were afraid above all of our former frankness.

I went to see my friend less frequently; then my visits almost ceased. More distant than a distracted stranger, she seemed insensible to everything that was not her mystical terror before the incomprehensible. And yet, she had been the pure sister to whom I had once confided all my dreams.

XVI

THE soil was reanimated under the kisses of winter. It laughed, like a happy giant, rejoiced by snow, wind and magnanimous frosts. The intoxications of the first cold spells filled the atmosphere with vigor and contentment . . .

Lorely was excited by the sharp frissons of the air. Her eyes shone, bluer, and her hair brightened to a more lively gold. Her pallor was traversed by pink tremors. She seemed a flower of ice and frost, and I was dazzled by her wintry beauty.

One evening, harsh with black ice, I happened to go past Ione's house, a house as closed to noises from outside as the abode of a hermit.

The desire to see once again the sweet friend of my amour-free past gripped me. Not without some hesitation—for the silence of the entire dwelling disconcerted me slightly—I rang the bell at the ungilded gate and crossed Ione's threshold.

I found her, as always, frightfully meditative. Her immeasurable forehead put a broad white glow in the gloomy room.

For a long time she bathed me with her unforgettably sad and tender eyes. I strove at first to decipher her gaze, but my reason lost itself there as in an abyss.

"I beg you," she murmured, in a very soft voice, "understand me. Divine what I can't yet tell you. Divine me and understand me . . ."

My impatient gesture was already responding to her.

"I can't divine you, Ione. I can't understand you. Help me . . ."

She shook her head slowly, with an expression of inexpressible regret.

"Let's talk about something else . . ."

She continued: "You're in love. You're not the person of old. You've renounced everything that was once your joy and your pride. You love Lorely. Your eyes are two dead lakes, and they only revive when they encounter her eyes. When she's far away, you still contemplate her and listen to her. You're no longer anything but a wandering shadow, you're no longer anything but the reflection and echo of Lorely."

A brief stupor froze me. For the first time, Ione was talking to me about my disastrous amour.

"You haven't found happiness . . ."

I tried to smile.

"No, certainly not. I have a soul so divinely unhappy that I wouldn't want to be consoled for anything in the world."

Ione uttered a long sigh.

"And yet, I have a prayer to address to you. I sense that I'm ill, and above all very tired. I'm soon going to repose in the beneficent Midi. Down there, there are fir trees with pink flowers, wisterias that fall all the way to the ground, olive groves the color of waves at twilight. In the mountains, the grass is blue with violets. Beds of algae turn the sea red. The sun there is so powerful that it dissipates all ills. Come down there. I'll cure you. As before, I'll be your consoler. Come down there . . ."

I thought that all the stars were going out at once in a miserable night. Quit Lorely, if only for a few hours! I almost smiled at the folly of the thought. The excessively suave image looked up in the depths of the evening. I saw again, in a décor of memory, the cruel blonde hair and the cruel blue eyes that rendered me so feeble and so cowardly . . .

I wanted to refuse the amicable offer affectionately. But I saw a supplication in Ione's eyes, and I dared not formulate the definitive sentence.

"Later," I replied. "I'll come later, Ione . . ."

I dared not look at my friend. A silence fell between us that seemed to extend eternally.

"You promise me to come?" said the pale Ione, finally. "You promise to come later?"

I lied resolutely.

"I promise you, darling."

"Weigh your words well. There's sometimes an ironic deity that obliges the accomplishment of promises made without the intention of keeping them . . ."

That light phrase, like a prophecy, fell into the shadow, still luminous.

I took hold of Ione's cold hands. The desolation that was weighing upon her oppressed me in my turn. We remained side by side, and a melancholy torpor enveloped us.

We were as sad as the dusk, and, like the dusk, we feared the imminent darkness, I have never known a more poignant hour than that dejected and fraternal hour.

XVII

IT was by solemn moonlight. There was expectation and veneration in the air. The silence was reminiscent of an august veil that no one had dared to lift.

Lorely's studio was open, as vast as a temple. When I went in, perfumed smoke was dissipating slowly there.

Lorely was folded up in an intense immobility. Finally, she stirred.

"This is the moonlight I was waiting for, in order to reveal myself to you," she said. "We need prayer and ecstasy around us."

Her words sounded like sacred music.

"You've only grasped confused appearances of me," she went on. "Tonight, you'll see me for the first time . . ."

She parted the curtain and the nocturnal light penetrated into the studio. There was no other illumination.

Long lilies stood up, springing from their silver vases like candles from their candelabra. Lorely started new perfumes burning in the cassolettes.

She advanced into the middle of the luminous space framed by shadow. With a ritual gesture, she let her garments fall. And my eyes marveled at all her splendor.

There was a radiation of immaculate flesh. I had never seen a female form more perfectly pure. The moonlight espoused that warm pallor amorously.

I knelt down. An exceedingly pure passion illuminated me serenely, Lorely's beauty was absolute; it transfigured desire and elevated it to the point of mystical adoration.

Around us, the silence was meditative. The lilies hurled their vehement perfume at Lorely. She and I were standing on the threshold of infinity. She was the priestess who, gradually, substituted herself for the indifferent idol. She was the divinized priestess. And I, the faithful disciple, was the soul chosen among all to adore her eternally. A light isolated us from the universe. Centuries could have passed without distracting me from my contemplation, without stealing my felicity: the light centuries would have passed over my forgetful forehead. And, priestess and disciple, she and I maintained our immutable attitudes and our fixed and religious souls.

XVIII

"AND yet, I would be able to love so enormously . . . !" Lorely's voice trailed an immeasurable regret.

"I would love with faith and with simplicity. I would annihilate myself entirely in that amour. I would no longer be artificial or eccentric; I would be like all women, the humblest and the most lamentable women, I who am haughty and joyful, and who toys with the love of others. I would no longer know the ennui of not suffering. I would hesitate, I would fear everything, I, who have never known either doubt or fear. I would be weak, I, who have always bent the will of others to my most futile caprice. And I would be grateful, with an unforgettable gratitude, to the woman who could make me love!"

Her distress carried me away and drowned me in a flood of bitterness. "But I fear never loving," she went on. "People irritate me, and disappoint me totally. They don't leave me the illusion necessary to amour."

She began to sob very quietly, like those who no longer have any hope.

"I shall never love," she said weeping. And looking at me through her tears: "How I envy you, you who suffer for amour!"

The light was declining. Lorely's tears shone in the twilight.

"Lorely," I implored, kneeling down beside her, "let me try to console you."

Very gently, she pushed me away.

"No. It's necessary to leave me alone, you see. I need silence in order to learn to resign myself."

I obeyed, and with a very heavy heart, I left her. I took the bleak path that led to an ancient Calvary.

Stupidly brutal hands had wrenched the Christ from the cross and broken it. Nothing any longer remained but the eternal cross, at the foot of which was a crumbling step corroded by the rain.

Prostrate in the shadow of that cross, her hair scattered, Doriane resembled the statue of a dead lover.

The desolation of her attitude was so poignant that at first I dared not approach her. Finally, I became bolder, and murmured:

"Doriane . . ."

She did not hear. I had to repeat, louder: "Doriane."

She parted the funereal hair that was streaming over her pale cheeks, and pronounced, in the one of those who have seen someone dear die: "I no longer hope."

"Have you lost your strength and your determination forever, then, Doriane?" I asked, in a tremulous voice.

"I've lost everything. Lorely will never love me."

I still lingered beside that suffering.

"What are you going to do, friend?"

She replied to me beneath her funereal tresses: "I'll leave."

"Oh, Doriane, who has become so cruelly dear to me, where will you go, then."

"I'll go towards empty spaces. I'll seek out places where there are no flowers, no verdure, no sounds of water, no women's voices. The sea will carry me far away from what I regret while fleeing it. It will rock me with its waves, appease me with its stellar calms. Perhaps I'll go to the desert strewn with mirages. Perhaps I'll go to the plains of infinite snow."

"Won't you ever come back among us, Doriane?"

"I'll come back when I've forgotten."

She fell silent, but resumed, in a minor key: "You love Lorely. You know, as I do, that the chagrins she inflicts are incurable."

"I know that, Doriane."

"Adieu," she said.

There was a stifled sob beneath the funereal tresses. Exhausted, Doriane had bumped her forehead on the stone step. And the Christless cross, the cross awaiting new martyrs, loomed up in the night.

XIX

I listened to the words that young women were exchanging in Lorely's studio.

"If it's true," said one of them, "that the soul puts on several human appearances, I was once born in Lesbos. I was only a paltry child devoid of grace, when a companion older than me took me into the temple where Psappha was invoking the goddess. I heard the ode to Aphrodita. The melodious memory was never extinguished over the years, nor through the centuries. However, I was only a taciturn child, and Psappha didn't love me. I loved her, and later, when I possessed feminine bodies, my sobs of desire went toward her. I was in Sicily when I learned of her death, but that death was so glorious that I didn't weep, and my companions' sobs surprised me and offended me. I reminded them of her magnanimous words: '. . . For it is not just that lamentations should be in the house of servants of the Muses; that is unworthy of us.'"

"Personally," mused the smiling Lorely, "I was a little Arab shepherd boy. I slept all day and only woke up at the approach of the green or violet night. Toward evening, following my flock, I returned from the mountain and I walked in the midst of a great red dust. Out there, I was the first to see the rising moon. I ran all the way to the

"

nearest village, proclaiming the moonrise. And all those
to whom I announced the great news looked at the sky
and rejoiced in seeing on the horizon the amber light that
precedes the moon . . .”

A young woman with a desirable amorous smile came
in and sat down at Lorely’s feet. Her gaze was raised and
her lips parted; her entire being offering and suppliant,
she adored her.

“Who is that young woman?” I asked.

“I don’t know anything about Nedda except that she’s
besotted with Lorely,” someone replied.

“Nedda!” I mused. “A fine childish and barbaric name.”

I drew closer to Lorely and Nedda, without their perceiving my presence.

Nedda murmured to Lorely: “I’ll never be cured of
you.”

And Lorely, in a voice more mysterious than the voice
of the breeze whispered to her: “I love you . . .”

She had forgotten the great thirst of her soul. She
seemed finally to be conquered, stolen. She smiled at the
irreflective tenderness that was offering itself to her.

“I love you,” she murmured, a second time.

Those words were sweeter to me than death, and cru-
eler than life itself. I abandoned myself to my miserable
joy. Lorely did not love me. But she loved that child.

Something deep down in me cried out, with a heart-
rending delight: “Lorely has discovered the amour for
which she was searching without hope.”

Nedda smiled at Lorely, and Lorely smiled at Nedda.

I turned away from them, because, in spite of everything, the sight of their sweet happiness tortured me. And

I forced myself to listen to the recitation that was being read in the shadow:

> *Happiness is a vast and noble as despair. It is necessary that your happiness frightens, like despair.*
>
> *The only true happiness is that of the hermit.*
>
> *It is necessary that happiness, like despair, is indifferent to all beings, to their speech and to their thoughts.*
>
> *I have only one example to propose to you: that of the woman in the ermine mantle. When her ermine mantle came unfastened and fell into the mud, passers-by picked it up and held it out to her, but with a haughty gesture, she turned away and went on her way, her shoulders bare under the wind and the rain.*
>
> *Refrain from moderation, as others refrain from excess. For prudence is the dangerous adversary of heroism and joy.*
>
> *Never follow advice, even one of those that I give. Everyone ought to live their personal life and earn the experience dearly that proves nothing.*
>
> *Sometimes, that which one imagines to be happiness is as gray as the twilight of sepulchers.*
>
> *Sometimes, too, I esteem that all happiness is cowardly and evil.*
>
> *But what is certain is that it is necessary to fear happiness like a treacherous friend who insinuates himself into the house. There are kinds*

of happiness that one only obtains in exchange for what is best and noblest in oneself. And one is then similar to a beggar who has torn out his eyes bloodily in exchange for silky garments and delicate feasts.

In truth, there is only one good: solitude.

There are few things to say about amour. No one knows it yet, although everyone thinks that she has experienced it.

What I tell you about amour might perhaps inspire a keen interest in you; nothing that concerns amour is indifferent to you. What I tell you about amour might perhaps interest you, but undoubtedly, you will not learn anything from it.

One is never sure of not loving. Nor is one ever sure of loving one day.

Listen respectfully to all those who speak to you about amour, and about their amour. For, in matters of amour, the words of a mediocre person might conceal a precious verity, an inestimable poetry.

The sole dolor without stars is that of individuals who suffer from not suffering.

Amity is more perilous than amour, for its roots are stronger and more profound than the roots of amour.

The dolor of amity is more bitter than the dolor of amour.

Certain individuals love amity, as others love amour. They suffer by virtue of amity as others do by virtue of amour. They only have one amity in their existence, as others only have one amour. It is in the hour when their amity escapes them that they finally despair.

And it is when they finally despair that they encounter happiness.

For happiness is like the magnificence of ruins.

Fear sleep, since it brings dreams heavy with fear, which cause one to bless the awakening, the gray awakening to oneself.

But do not fear death.

For the dead, lying on a bed of violets, are no longer saddened by the dreams that existence has not realized, nor vanished perfumes, nor music that has been killed.

For the dead have lost the cruel memory of the amity that once deceived them and the amour that once betrayed them . . .

Lorely and Nedda were not listening to the recitation. Both of them, having slid into the circle that surrounded the poet, nevertheless remained isolated in their tender felicity. I understood that they were thus maintaining around them, in the midst of the noisiest crowd, an amorous solitude.

Lorely's blonde hair, unfastened, mingled with Nedda's brown hair. Nedda's brown eyes sank into Lorely's blue eyes. Outside the world, their souls espoused one another.

I had the vision of a pool on which Lethean nenuphars were slumbering. The sun disappeared over the horizon. And eternity seemed buried in the depths of that dead water . . .

Beneath the dead water and the nenuphars, two ephemerae were whirling, whose iridescent wings scintillated in the setting sun. Never had any nacre, never had any rainbow, equaled the changing splendor of those wings.

I considered the ephemerae with a sad wonder, knowing that the end of their amour was imminent. But, rising higher still, I saw them resplendent, incomparable . . .

Gradually, those ephemerae grew. Their radiance was augmented. And they were two women who were embracing, recklessly. They rose above the silence and the nothingness, and, before disappearing, they united their feverish lips in a vain amorous kiss . . .

XX

LATER, Lorely said to me, speaking about Nedda:
"I nearly loved her. She still loves me . . ."

In the eyes of my deceptive Undine, I read both compassion and envy. She went on:

"I'm striving to give her the belief and the happiness that escape me. I resemble those actors who put on make-up and a royal mantle every evening for the illusion and the joy of others. When the play is over, how sadly they go home, poor even in the soul, through the icy streets, covered in the rags that their life has left them!"

There was a funeral march in my soul, punctured by a knell.

Lorely had forgotten my presence. Talking to herself, she added:

"It's necessary to envy slaves. Myself, I'm free, terribly free . . ."

XXI

AGAIN, I went into Ione's house.

I was astonished to see my friend clad in gray cloth like that of nuns, whose pleats fell around her with a religious severity.

The unique ruby was no longer bleeding on her neck. The ruby belt no longer espoused the frail stem of her waist. The ample red velvet dress no longer surrounded her with its ardent reflections, which evoked, for me, beautiful evenings in Florence.

There had been a mysterious transformation in Ione. However, I did not sense that she was happy yet.

"I've just spent a strange and almost supernatural week in the depths of a humble country convent," she told me. "I went there to repose my soul a little. All week long I was bathed in divine simplicity . . ."

She stopped, in order to remember better.

"A very young sister, in which the naivety of the former peasant girl persisted, came to talk to me in the exquisite cold bare cell in which I lived. I had never imagined anything as purely admirable as that young sister. She had a grateful and replete soul. For, possessing nothing on earth, she had received all the treasures of heaven . . ."

Ione's eyes were burning with a supernatural flame.

"She coveted nothing on earth. She did not even perceive the magnificence of landscapes, the sea or the sun, she who dwelt in the shadow of the chapel or the cell. She lived a narrow life, a life in jail. She was ignorant of music or verses. She was ignorant of all terrestrial beauty. And she was happy. Can you understand the profound significance of those simple words: *she was happy?* She had found, effortlessly, what we all pursue so bitterly and which we all seek with so much vain ingenuity. In truth, what we dream of through pleasures, luxury and travel, that little sister retained ingenuously in her obscure and poor cloister."

Tears trickled down Ione's pale cheeks.

"She believed. Or, rather, she knew. Isn't knowing being ignorant of everything?"

"Perhaps," I said, hesitantly.

"That little peasant sister was a living miracle. She was ugly, with a beautiful smile. She always had on her lips the words: *God is very good.*"

Ione went on:

"And that convent appeared to me such a nocturnal haven in which all the calm stars were reflected. My soul went to run aground in that definitive peace. I didn't go about thinking any longer; I went about believing, like that little saint with the plebeian face and the rough hands. And I dare to hope that I'll be happy, like her."

"Ione, my friend . . ."

"Oh, the dear sisters, who don't want anything on earth, whose joys and wealth are not of this earth. Oh, the dear little country saint!"

"Ione," I said, "why didn't you stay in the convent?"

"Doubt chased me away, terrible doubt: the doubt that is killing me."

"But can't you return one day to that haven, that refuge of souls?"

"If faith is finally accorded to me, I'll return there forever."

"You've already adopted the robe. Your stride is the patient tread of nuns . . ."

She divined my thought and blushed slightly.

"I've given my ruby belt to the Superior, in order that she can sell it for the poor. My adornments no longer procured me the slightest joy. I wanted them to give joy to others . . ."

Ione sighed.

"If only, one day, I receive the inestimable gift of faith! I'm searching so ardently that I must discover it one day . . ."

"Ione," I said, "It's necessary to desire it with less anguish in order to receive it, as one receives the host, in a profound peace, with eyes closed and hands crossed over the breast."

Ione's lips parted, as if to receive the white host.

"Could I, in the example of the sisters, carry all infinity within me? If you knew of what splendor their souls are made! Most of them are divinely puerile; they live outside the century, like children in a garden of lilies. They have ignorant and charmed smiles. And others have gazes that have sounded eternity and space. All are equally dear to the pensive Madonna and the dolorous Christ."

Ione stopped. And I saw in imagination, as she did in memory, the little saint with the plebeian face and rough hands, the little peasant saint . . .

XXII

ALL the light entered into the room, a light so intense that the eyes were dazzled by it.

Ione had entered with the light. Her hair and her eyes were radiant. A felicity emanated from her. And I saw her laughing in the daylight.

"Light," she said, "light! Don't you feel, as much as I do, the power of that great word, which tears the darkness and descends, with grace, into the depths of the heart?"

I could only find these poor words: "Finally, finally, you're happy, Ione . . ."

Her only response was to turn the glory of her face toward me.

"I've received faith as one receives the host, eyes closed and hands crossed over the breast. I only feel sad in returning to the sentiment of reality, in falling back to earth. I'm so weary of human anguish and ugliness!"

"You're speaking as if you no longer desired anything but death, Ione."

"For me, death will be the beginning of a paradisal life."

"In that case, my dear Ione, my sweet Ione, my sister and my companion of all times, may you soon find the death that is your most beautiful desire."

As I spoke, I held back the tears that rose to my eyes. I saw Ione exhausted, in spite of her courage, exhausted by the long doubts of old. She could not live. She retained within her a soul avid for eternity, and would never be content with poor mortal tenderness, brief and uncertain tenderness.

In a surge of fraternal pity, I said to her: "May you soon attain the death of which you dream!"

Ione finally possessed faith. And faith illuminated the hard road that she was following, stumbling. But the brightest light cannot triumph over the prostration that exhausts the limbs or the ennui of the monotonous route . . .

"Do you believe in miracles?" Ione asked.

"I believe in everything that isn't real."

"And do you believe in visions?" she interrogated. "I mean, interior visions."

Immediately, she perceived that I did not understand, and went on: "I think that the Most Holy Virgin and the gentle Savior manifest themselves in our souls when we summon them. One hears them, and one even sees them. But one sees them in oneself, one hears them in the utmost depths of oneself. They're resplendent, not before the eyes but in the tremulous heart. It's thus that Mary revealed herself to me yesterday, and spoke to me in the chapel, where miracles have been accomplished before."

"I know that chapel, whose shadow is so mysterious that one has no difficulty in admitting the accomplishment of miracles there."

"I was kneeling there in broad daylight. The sun was as penetrating as it is where we are. The air was blue and limpid. There was no disturbance, no enigma. And it's in that simplicity, in that great light, that the miracle was accomplished quite naturally."

She went on, in a lower voice: "A light rose up in my soul. That light was so fragrant, so musical, that I understood . . . That light was the Virgin herself. And an interior voice made itself heard, a voice that was hers. That voice said to me: Don't weep any longer. Soon you'll be consoled. Soon, Ione, you're going to die . . ."

I uttered a cry.

"I left the chapel," Ione continued. "I was very calm. I've never been as calm. Yes, I was crying within me the peace that surpasses all human peace. It's necessary not to be astonished by miracles, for miracles are very simple things . . ."

I listened with a silent respect. I sensed that Ione was telling the truth: that the vision had spoken to her in the chapel full of sunlight, and that the vision had not abused her.

Perhaps the eyes of the sick see further and more distinctly. Perhaps . . .

No one will ever know. It's necessary to bow one's head before the inexplicable, if one does not believe, like Ione . . .

Knowing that she was going to die, I considered her with all my lamentable tenderness. And I had the childish temptation to fall to my knees before her, weeping. But one thought consoled me: *She's happy. It's necessary not to trouble her superhuman felicity.*

Ione looked at me, all the way to the soul. "May the light that has dazzled me completely illuminate you one day," she said.

And on those words of hope, she quit me.

I wept until nightfall. And during the night, I had enough strength and determination to rejoice with Ione over her imminent death.

XXIII

I learned that Nedda, having discovered the truth, had fled the house where Lorely had held her enlaced.

Nedda had run away. Her illusions had collapsed one by one. She could no longer lie to herself, and Lorely had not been able to play her difficult role to the end. Gradually, very slowly, their arms had come apart.

It was the slow agony of the end of an amour; finally, there was the abrupt tear, the rupture.

And I encountered Nedda by the side of another woman . . .

That other woman did not have the morbid charm of Lorely. She was neither Undine nor Viviane; she was only a vulgar woman. But Nedda was walking pressed against her, and their two bodies sought one another, drawing together unconsciously.

I stopped the two companions and I said to Nedda: "Oh, Nedda, can one really love a second time, when one has loved?"

She threw her arms around the neck of the vulgar woman, whose short-cropped hair framed a low brow. And Nedda said to me, in a passionate tone: "See how I love her!"

The vulgar woman, who had known numerous amours, said then: "I've never loved a woman as I love Nedda today."

They joined their lips.

But all that passion was affirmed too loudly. They loved one another with too much bitter determination. Veritable amours are made of silence.

While I reflected thus, Nedda, having separated from her companion, came to me.

"I'm happy," she threw at me, as a challenge.

I did not know what to reply.

She protested, rebelling against my mute incredulity.

"I love her," she affirmed, pointing her finger at her companion, who was waiting for her, lying amid the deep russet grass.

"Don't you ever think about Lorely?" I dared to ask.

She hesitated, and stammered: "Sometimes . . . oh, yes, sometimes . . . but I love elsewhere, and, as you see, I'm happy."

"One doesn't forget Lorely."

"But my new friend adores me, and Lorely no longer loves me. I even think that she never loved me."

"Who knows, Nedda?"

"Don't you think that my new companion is charming in all respects? I chose her, you see, because she bears no resemblance to . . . the other. Isn't that so?"

"In fact, she scarcely resembles her."

"She's differently blonde, a less unreal blonde. She doesn't have Lorely's lunar pallor."

"In fact, she has the round pink cheeks of young Flemish women."

"And her short-cropped hair amuses me. Sometimes, when I'm kissing her, I surprise myself blushing, as if I were kissing an overly bold boy."

"You're right, she does entirely resemble a boy."

"This one won't smile with a smile that promises and dissimulates. This one won't murmur words that are distressing to hear, words that are lies because they're too beautiful."

"Undoubtedly."

"This one will simply love me. I'm so tired of everything that's complicated. I'm very happy. When you see Lorely again, tell her that I'm happy."

"I'll repeat to her what you've just told me."

"Thank you. Look, over there, my companion is making me a sign to go back to her. I'm running to join my dear beloved. *Au revoir!*"

Lightly, she ran away.

I wandered in a little wood, where white violets were hiding jealously in unknown corners of verdure. And I meditated on Lorely and on Nedda, and on the poor ephemeral amour of Lorely and Nedda . . .

XXIV

O NE DAY, Lorely had rejected my desolate amour with a colder cruelty. As she left, she had thrown nasty laughter at me. And her gaze persisted within me, like a blue blade plunged into my flesh.

When I went in, I had told her about my resolution to leave for the Midi the following day, where I was to see Ione . . . Ione, who only had a short time to live.

When she knew that I was able to leave her for a few months, Lorely lashed me with bitter laughter.

Hours had gone by. I waited for her in the studio, where the echo of that nasty laughter still resonated.

My face had become fixed, like faces of stone. One might have thought that for many years, perhaps centuries, I had been motionless in that same spot. My eyelids had become heavy, my jaws weighty, and all my limbs seemed paralyzed.

I was stifling. Abruptly, I went out and I wandered in the garden.

I headed toward an arbor of wisteria, where Lorely had the custom of sitting. Suddenly the murmur of voices became audible. It was Lorely's voice, and that of a man. I heard the voice of the man saying, ardently: "I love you."

Lorely replied, musically: "I'm glad that you love me."

Then the man said: "Do you love me? Do you love me?"

And Lorely said, with a perfidious softness: "I love you . . ."

The man fell at Lorely's knees. Undulating, she rose to her feet and escaped him, as she had once slipped out of my embrace. At a very slow pace, they drew away.

Time passed, confusedly.

And I began to think.

Certainly, Lorely had lied just now. Certainly, Lorely did not love, could not love, that man. Phrases pronounced in the past returned in memory.

"Has a woman ever loved a man? I can scarcely conceive such an aberration. The fact of yielding to the masculine yoke appears to me as a monstrous thing, an unnatural passion . . ."

But then, why had she murmured, with her Florentine lips, that vile and degrading lie?

I no longer understood. That she had neglected my taciturn presence for the veiled smiles of beautiful young women, was very explicable and infinitely pardonable. But how had she dared make confessions to that man?

She was profaning herself, diminishing herself miserably. How, and why, was she, my virginal priestess, playing that infamous comedy?

I no longer understood . . .

XXV

I wandered through the streets, where a mauve dusk was reddening, like a violet fabric, when the Annunciatrix appeared beside me.

She spoke to me in these terms:

"I shall reveal to you the soul of the woman you have loved without ever understanding her.

"Lorely takes pleasure in making men suffer by the impudent offer of her inviolable beauty. For it's agreeable to her to know that she is inaccessible in a brutal atmosphere of desire and covetousness.

"Lorely adores the tortures to which her smile and her gaze give birth. The sentiment of her feminine power intoxicates her. But she does not love the men whom it pleases her to cause to suffer."

The Annunciatrix turned away, ready to leave.

"An advice!" I implored. "An advice, to light my path . . ."

As she drew away, she said to me: "I'll return to you when the time comes."

XXVI

I dared to make dolorous reproaches to Lorely. I dared to criticize her for the confessions of the man, overheard by chance. Finally, I dared to criticize her for her deceitful response.

Undisturbed, she let fall: "By what right do you speak to me in that fashion, you whom I don't love?"

She went on, implacably: "And since I don't love you, let's separate. Know that I've always been honest with you. Have I lavished false protestations of tenderness upon you? From the first moment, I opened the emptiness of my heart to you. I would have liked to love you, but you have not been able to inspire in me the amour that I desired so vainly."

She died, in a melancholy fashion: "The amour that I shall never find."

And she disappeared, in a sad frisson.

XXVII

I opened the telegram. A few words that summarized brutally the tragedy of a soul:

Ione gravely ill. Come.

And I left for the Midi, where Ione was dying.

XXVIII

I went through Ione's garden, where white irises were paling, as sad and pure as lilies. I shall remember those white irises throughout my human existence. A melancholy scent of violets lingered in the pathways, like an adieu.

Something articulated clearly: *You are going to lose Ione. Ione is going to die.*

And I listened without understanding yet.

I picked a white iris. I said: "This flower is going to die, like Ione. It is already dying, like Ione. It is dead, like Ione . . ."

I went into the house, which had already taken on the ashen color of funereal dwellings. And someone told me, weeping, that Ione had just died.

XXIX

I remember that, in my room, the blinking of my eyelids enfevered my sick eyes. I became heavily, stupidly drowsy, like a drunken man lying on stones.

. . . And I woke up . . . The room was blue with darkness.

Ione, standing at the foot of my bed, was contemplating her hands, in her familiar attitude. Then she retreated to a corner where she was no longer anything but a whiteness of mist and dream.

I tried to get up and go toward her. My foot slipped and I fell into a flow of hot lava that was streaming and seething at the foot of my bed. I wanted to cry out in distress, but the fuming river carried me away, a wisp of straw adrift in its fiery waves. To either side of the blazing torrent, old women were crouching, cooking rice and eggs over the liquid flame. And the moon was coppery, like a winter sun. Ashes were falling in a dense hail.

An abominable thirst desiccated my palate and throat.

. . . My eyes opened in a temple to the breath of a furnace. A ruby throne reddened the darkness like a setting star. From the height of the throne, Kali contemplated me with a religious ferocity. She dropped the skull that she was crushing in the manner of a hungry bitch, and smiled at me with her red teeth . . .

The sirocco carried me away, a whirlwind of burning and yellow dust, filling my bruised lungs. The sand and the dust were choking me, blinding me, burying me . . .

Then there was a childishly artificial landscape, which evoked the English illustrations of Norwegian and German fairy tales. Varnished trees with painted foliage were aligned to either side of a path smoother than a little girl's hair . . .

And I found myself before Lorely's corpse. Lorely was floating on a stagnant marsh. Her pale breasts were two nenuphars. The revulsed eyes were looking at me. She was floating, her hair mingled with irises and reeds, like a perverse Ophelia. And with her eyes, devoid of a gaze, she contemplated me eternally . . .

I felt the cold air of a mortuary crypt on my face. I was standing in the middle of four coffins. The largest was a man's coffin. There was something massive and imposing about it. I understood that it was the coffin of an important man, a master of the hour. Flowers devoid of poetry were displayed there in large dark patches: immortelles and heavy pansies with red velvet petals.

Beside that mass, attenuated and diminutive, was an embryonic coffin, the coffin of a larva, bathing in the twilight of limbo. Colorless wreaths, with a very faint scent, were fading there with simplicity. That child's coffin was tragic and null, like everything that might have been.

Frightful funerary stained glass covered a shrunken coffin, the wood of which was furrowed by numerous wrinkles, like cobwebs. Those hideous wreaths of black and yellow pearls were to perpetuate the bourgeois memory of an old woman with a surly voice.

And in the deepest shadow, in a perpetual adoration of fervent candles, there was a virginal coffin perfumed by white violets. I understood that I was seeing Ione's coffin.

The silence was so mysterious that even my heartbeats had fallen silent.

But, more frightful than the clarion of divine judgment, the wood of the large coffin was creaking. That was the fermentation of putrescence.

A gasp, and another gasp, and a final gasp . . . I had ceased to exist. I was a soul stripped of its body, a formless and confused mass, devoid of limits and consistency, which was floating, having no other sensation than a shiver of nudity.

A prayer surfaced in the milieu of that self-conscious void: "A personality! A body! A name! Oh, to become someone! To be what I was, although I have already forgotten who I was!"

Darkness . . . and nothingness . . .

XXX

FINALLY, dawn rose in my darkness, and the gray apparition of beings and things replaced the fears of delirium.

I was about to see the dead person that I loved . . .

Ione was reposing in a funeral crypt. Her narrow coffin was adorned with white violets.

I remained among the dead all day, and only withdrew toward nightfall. The perfume of dying flowers mingled with I know not what insipid odor, which frightened me. At intervals, the wood of the coffins creaked in the silence, with a very soft sound.

When I went back up into the light, everything that I saw seemed incomprehensible and new to me. Voices surprised me with their strange sonorities, the rumble of the carriages in the streets astonished me, and the sight of people struck me with stupor.

One day, someone came to tell me that the funeral would take place the following day.

In a mist of tears, I remember the church, and the compassionate crowd, and a few profound dolors. I can see again the white catafalque and the virginal flowers. I can also evoke the cold British clergyman and the cold Anglican service. In spite of Ione's conversion to the

Catholic religion, her parents had imposed their will in the choice of Protestant ceremonies.

The cry of resurrection and eternity sounded hollow before the coffin, where the pale flowers were fading. I heard, like a knell dominating the sobs, the liturgical phrase:

Though worms shall eat this body . . .

And the horrible vision of that soft and delicate body prey to the worms of the sepulcher surged forth to my eyes . . .

Though worms shall eat this body . . .

Those words resounded within me more profoundly than all the promises of immortality.

I fell to my knees. Before whom, before what, and why? I don't know. I simply knelt down, before something that was above my dolor, and which I did not understand . . .

XXXI

MY heart desolate, my soul more desolate still, I went to Lorely's house. She alone could enlighten, could embalm compassionately, my miserable darkness.

With a heart-rending hope, I knocked on the door . . . And received no response.

XXXII

I left the next day for Toledo. How I love that autumnal city, the leprosy of its houses, the malady of its pavements, the wounds of its walls, the agony of its frescoes!

The memory returned to me of a morbid melody composed in honor of Our Lady of Fevers, so victoriously mounted in a reliquary in that city of desolation . . .

> *Your fetid breath has corrupted the city . . .*
> *A green of gangrene, a green of poison*
> *Swarms, and night crawls like a reptile.*
> *The crowd recites a prayer in chorus,*
> *A fervent delirium burning the lips,*
> *A glacial frisson amid the sweat,*
> *Toward your lividity, Our Lady of Fevers!*
>
> *Shadow has consecrated its evil gleam to you,*
> *The blue phosphors are your frail candles,*
> *And the fire follets gild your altar,*
> *Virgin who smiles at the death of virgins,*
> *Who remains deaf to the obscure appeal,*
> *Madonna to whom matins and vespers*
> *Rise up shivering, Our Lady of Leprosies!*

Your cathedral, with walls corroded by lichens
Sickens the evening with its vapid warmth.
On the soiled beds of hideous couplings,
The moisture of sick hands sweats.
Scaly lepers and the moribund
Mingle their sighs with the shrieks of ospreys
And kiss your knees, Our Lady of Wounds!

Your tragic elect have inclined their foreheads
Beneath the divine wind of your litanies.
And amid the incense and the sacred songs
And the flow of acrid fluids,
Exhales a reek of pestilence.
The pus and the blood and pale tears
Have blessed your naked feet, Our Lady of Gasps!

Gradually, I discerned the cruel pallor of the Madonna of plagues. In her stagnant eyes, the reflections of dead waters were tinted with blue and green. Paludal breaths emanated from the tormented pleats of her robe. Her face was as tumultuous as the visions of delirium. And I recognized in the mortal image the image of Lorely. The stagnant eyes reflected Lorely's eyes. The changing face was similar to Lorely's face. Lorely had come to corrupt the air and the sunlight, to corrupt forever my hopes of forgetfulness and cure. She had come, knowing that I would not escape her.

The days went by, and I wrote to a friend with androgynous hands in order to abridge a dolorous hour.

She haunts me like a remorse. I can no longer
get a grip on myself, I can no longer revive. Her
memory is killing me without finishing me off.

In vain I have tried to kill myself twice. If I find in the depths of my weakness and my cowardice, however, the energy to disappear, if I finally succeed, you will never, ever tell Lorely, will you, that she alone dealt me the final blow?

The very pure amity of Ione was once my consolation and my refuge. Since her disappearance, I no longer have anything on earth.

The fortnight that followed my first encounter with Lorely was nothing but an ecstatic stupor, an enchanted splendor. And yet I knew that she did not love me, that I was deceiving myself, as she was also deceived.

It is not her fault if she could not love me. Nor is it mine. Do not blame her, since I do not blame her myself.

I hate life. I do not know how or why I still exist.

Everything that I write is futile, weak, and impotent: as impotent as my thought, as weak as my heart, and as futile as my life.

I rejoice in the memory of Ione's death. I am triumphant in the certainty of her repose. She is no longer suffering the oppression of existence, she is no longer anything but a perfume drifting in the depths of the night, a drop of sap in a blade of grass . . .

Dolor! Oh, the banality and the monotony of dolor! It is vulgar, since it belongs to everyone. It is the graceless prostitute that the crowd possesses. For having known it, there remains to me a lassitude mingled with disgust . . .

Lorely! She has divine soulful smiles and unexpected tears. But above all, she has implacable cruelties. I want to love her as one loves a dead woman. I only want to think any longer about the incomparable that is in her, and the sadness of a few tender hours.

She was my first amour, you see; I have only ever loved her. I believe that I shall never be able to love another woman with that same furious and wild passion.

I cannot forget her in the hours when I want to distract myself from that obsession. I have paid discreet court to a Spanish woman with the feet of an infanta, but that is only a game devoid of importance, a simple theme of conversation on which it is more agreeable to embroider than on the excessively worn theme of rain and fine weather. It resembles true love as the pain of a child resembles the agony of a martyr.

Doesn't it?

I dream of a death that would be a sensuality, a death that would be a consolation for life, the impossible happiness itself. The obsession with that death is like a desire that is exalted toward a beloved woman . . .

Shortly thereafter, the friend with the androgynous hands addressed a letter to me in which she gently mocked my inconstancy.

I replied to her:

Do you not know, friend, that psychology is mistaken almost as infallibly as medicine? You have fallen into the most profound error in believing that my love for Lorely is conjugated in the past. Everything is finished between us; that is the best of the reasons why I adore her.

As for the Sevillan with the feet of an infanta, O grossly abused seeress, I shall see her again tomorrow after a week's absence, and that thought is utterly indifferent to me. She has the perfidy of the other, the Unique, without the charm and the magic of the entire being that once ensorcelled me.

Perhaps I am telling you all this lightly. The truth is that I am adrift in dolor. I hate Lorely passionately. I would see her suffer with delight; and yet I would give my brain and my blood to spare her the slightest anguish. I can do no more. I love her.

Au revoir, my dear friend. Until when? I don't know. I can't envisage the future when the present has such a dolorous intensity. Perhaps you'll feel a little sorry for me, since you're as loyal a friend as you are subtle, and entirely delightful when you don't indulge in psychology.

I dare not kiss your hands. You have hands that are almost virile, hands that possess, which grasp and hold, but never let go. I have, as you know, a passion for hands, which are more eloquent than faces.

I remember how Ione, for hours on end, contemplated her unhealthy hands with the dullness of old ivory . . .

Nor do I dare shake your hand as a comrade, for you have perverse hands and they disconcert me. Long, sinuous fingers make me too anxious. All things considered, I will quite simply bid you: Au revoir.

I left Toledo in order to plunge myself into the Moorish dream. The Alhambra was a pious enchantment for me. The *Sala de las Dos Hermanos* became dearer to me than all the rest. By a kind of sortilege of memory, I saw the two royal sisters Zorayda and Zorahayda.[1]

They were sitting facing one another on either side of the fountain. The singing water was shining in the shadow, and their eyes were thoughtful as they contemplated it. The immutable reverie of the guzla players fell asleep less harmoniously. Sometimes, the princesses intoned a bizarre chant, and their voices dominated the music of the fountain.

Their gazes, simultaneously close and distant, sought one another through a cool mist. But the fountain separated them from one another more efficaciously than all the doors of the palace. The fountain seemed to them to be an insurmountable obstacle. They smiled at one another through the mist of water. They never dared to sit down next to one another and hold hands, and they died without destroying in their souls the infinite charm of desire and regret.

---

1 Zorayda and Zorahayda are most familiar in English as characters in Washington Irving's "Legend of the Three Beautiful Princesses" in *Tales of the Alhambra* (the third princess is Zayda).

XXXIII

TOWARD the end of winter I tore myself away from the marvelous city and returned to Paris, with the cowardly hope of seeing again, for a moment, the fugitive beauty of Lorely.

I was unable to find her.

It was one of those evenings when Lorely should have come, an evening of moonlight and stars, which would have been inexpressibly beautiful if she had come . . .

And I thought that I was similar to a man returning from a marshy country, carrying in his marrow and his bones the fever of which, one day, he would die.

One hides that patient fever within oneself, almost without suspecting it, and hardly feeling it, which is able to bide its time. It accords an illusory respite, artificially, and one imagines that one no longer has anything to fear for from it; but it will not allow one to escape it. And one night, one finds it at one's bedside . . .

Thus I rediscovered the thought of Lorely, the piercing, mortal thought of Lorely.

One does not forget . . . One never forgets . . .

It was one of those evenings when she should have come . . .

XXIV

THE night was milky with a strange starlight. A diffuse light fell from the sky. And, a pure breath of wind having parted the curtains, all the light of the stars was snowing in my bedroom.

I was only half-asleep. I was drifting between the real and the dream, like the thrice sacred coffin floating between the earth and the sky.

A dream blossomed behind my eyelids . . .

I was wandering in a vast field circled by a motionless river. Nenuphars were dormant on its surface. Those nenuphars were white and wide open. They spread an odor of slumber around them. I stopped to pick the meadow narcissi, which were delicately blonde, like little yellow lilies. Crocuses and primroses were also paling in the field, where there were neither cicadas nor bees.

I did not see any trees or hills on the horizon. I only saw the vast field of pale grass, where the meadow narcissi and the primroses were growing.

Around me, a meditative silence expanded, which one might have thought woven of memories. The daylight was faint, but persistent. A mist clung to the horizon like an immense cobweb.

Suddenly, little vapors formed on the motionless surface on which the nenuphars were dormant, and ran, diaphanously. I followed them with my eyes. A weeping willow inclined, as if to seek in the water the forgotten reflection of a vanished image.

I perceived two women coming toward me, walking slowly. One was dressed in emerald green and carrying a palm. Her reddish-brown hair fell over her shoulders. The second was dressed in dark red. She was holding a cithara. Her hair, the color of ruddy flax, was imprisoned by a golden net.

Both of them were clad in a very ancient fashion. Their pointed shoes were embroidered with bizarre designs. Those golden embroideries sparkled through the grass.

They passed before me without turning their heads, without addressing a word to me. Their gaze was so distracted that I dared not stop them. At a distance, I took the same route as them . . .

The two unknown women walked at a measured pace, as if they were accomplishing an august rite. They walked alongside the river, straight and sacerdotal.

The field seemed to be infinite. It extended monotonously, sometimes receding like space itself.

The unknown women joined a group of musiciennes. Some, with Egyptian adornments, were seated, as rigidly as Isis. Kinnors were silent between their fingers. Others, in white peplums, were watchful beside their dormant lyres. Others were leaning over lutes. A woman in a hieratic robe was seated before an organ.

All the instruments were mute. No sound troubled the still air. And yet, arranged around the musiciennes, young women with robes of all centuries and all countries were listening in ecstatic attitudes. They were listening with their eyes, listening with all their leaning bodies.

At my approach, however, as if I had interrupted an aerial concert, the musiciennes and their listeners stood up abruptly, with gestures and expressions of anger. They all got up and they all fled. Green, orange and violet trains brushed the grass.

I followed the fugitives with my eyes. They dispersed in the mist suspended at the extremity of the field like a vast cobweb.

I found myself alone. A few instants shelled out their grains of sand . . . A veiled form suddenly emerged from the distant mist.

An inexplicable peace, an incomprehensible happiness, floated over me, like two doves. I awaited the arrival of that form, preceded by fumes of water . . .

A closed nenuphar blossomed as if by a miracle. The veiled form advanced . . . with inexpressible thrills of ecstasy, in a radiant dolor, I recognized Ione . . .

I knelt down. And, in a prayer or a sob, my soul was exhaled toward the Resuscitated.

Speech expired on my lips; but tears sprang from my heart and streamed inexhaustibly.

"Ione . . ." I murmured. "My dear Ione . . . my sweet Ione . . . my poor beloved . . ."

Something deep down within me warned me of the unreality of such a dolorous happiness.

This joy is illusory. This joy will not endure . . .

Ione was considering me, however, with her sad and tender eyes. Oh, the same eyes as of old! Oh, the same gaze!

And as small, very tiny, chances take on an incalculable importance when it is a matter of those we love, I saw that she was wearing the red dress of old, the same robe that evoked for me beautiful evenings in Florence.

Although the Resuscitated was very close to me, I sensed obscurely that she was still infinitely distant.

There was an unfathomable silence between us.

I contemplated Ione with my avid eyes, my bewildered pupils, which had finally found her again. A meadow narcissus brushed her dress. A sunbeam played over her long archangelic hands.

The suffering of that moment was so profound, and so acute, that I could not endure it any longer. I extended my suppliant hand and tried to touch a pleat of the red dress . . . the red dress of old . . .

But the Apparition vanished immediately. The pale field, the river, and the mist disappeared . . .

In my bruised soul, Ione died for a second time . . .

XXXV

I felt in the utmost depths of being the sadness of spring. That revolt of young plants against imminent death, that futile effort of life, oppressed me like suffering. How many memories in the heart of renewals!

I was walking around an opaline lake, my eyes vaguely charmed by the play of foliage over the water, when a limpid voice made me shudder. I recognized Dagmar, a young poet whom I had once admired for her delicate coloring of old Saxe. Her curly hair haloed her with child-like grace, and her eyes, a puerile blue, opened wide, as if ecstasized by a tale of enchantment.

"How somber you are in this beautiful sunlight!" she said, her bright eyes smiling.

"The joy of others saddens my egotism, Dagmar."

She considered me compassionately.

"And Lorely? A year ago you were her guard dog, meaning no offense."

"Oh, have no fear, I still have the cult of the absurd. I haven't forgotten Lorely; it's Lorely who has lost the memory of my modest existence."

"You must have suffered a great deal. You no longer have the same face. I hesitated for a moment before recognizing you. I'm very good, fundamentally, in spite of my eccentric humor of a spoiled child. I'll listen to the tale of your woes, even if it's interminable. It's the best means of cure. By dint of talking about something, one ends up becoming detached from it, for one wearies even of one's dearest dolors."

"Perhaps you're right, little April eglantine. But you're frightening me slightly; you resemble the morning too much."

"Morning is very mild when it rises after a feverish night," she said. "It's necessary not to fear the morning. I've seen it wandering in the boscage, to see whether the red roses were open during the night. And with an infinitely compassionate gesture, it appeases the long insomnia of tobacco flowers, which finally go to sleep, one by one."

"Sleep . . ." I murmured. "It's such a long time since I've enjoyed veritable slumber. I've learned to love in insomnias that bring me nocturnal thoughts so different from the thoughts of the day, and the very clear perception of invisible presences. Ione sometimes returns during the silence of midnights. Her Florentine dress, her dark red velvet dress seems a reflection of the setting sun in the depths of the darkness. She gazes at her pale hands. She has such beautiful and gentle hands, the hands of a sister and a consoler. But her eyes are always lowered, and she never murmurs a single word."

"Don't think about the dead. Let the dead bury their dead."

"It's because I'm closer to the dead than the living, Dagmar. How I love your name of a daughter of the North! A name more vigorous than the sea breeze; a fresh and joyful name, in your resemblance. The names of women are sometimes strangely evocative . . ."

Dagmar was not listening to me.

She went on: "I adore tales of enchantment. When I was little, my wooden horse lifted me up, a fabulous charger, toward the distances where the elves were playing in the moonlight. I've kept the soul of a child, astonished by the fantastic stories told on long winter evenings."

"You're charming, Dagmar. I'll come with you with great pleasure. If it's true that every person finds their image in the animal kingdom, you resemble a hummingbird."

"And what does Lorely resemble?" the curious child asked, her eyes shining.

"A wild swan."

A heavy sadness circled my forehead, like a band of darkness.

"How many people have you loved on earth?" asked the young poet, in order to deflect the course of my imagination.

"I've loved in amity, and my pure sister is dead. I've loved amorously, and that was a disaster. Today, Dagmar, I love solitude."

"Well, you'll forsake it for me. Come to see me tomorrow."

I promised . . .

. . . I went to see Dagmar the next day, less sad for having seen the freshness of her smile. The little princess had put on a dress of slightly barbaric brightness. Like all young people, she liked things that were resplendent and sparkling. Around her neck, a row of large turquoises resembled the necklace of a savage girl.

"Look," she exclaimed, "the lilac is just flowering in the garden. Let's go see the tortoise, whose ancient wisdom is meditating amid the verdure. It's belated, like benevolence. It might have thousands of years of existence, and people have believed them to be eternal. Look. It's so attentive and so taciturn that it seems to be listening to the grass growing and the roots plunging into the ground. Sometimes, it seems harmonious . . ."

"And doubtless is," I confirmed. "Didn't Hermes form the first lyre with the shell of a tortoise? And didn't Psappha say: 'Come, divine tortoise, and become melodious beneath my fingers . . .' I have the greatest veneration for tortoises."

Dagmar stroked my arm. The sun gilded her childlike curls. She smiled at me, and a sudden wild tenderness burned in my soul for that creature of sap and dew. I was thirsty for her, as for blue water of the dawn.

And the brutal desire to bite those lips naively offered for a kiss became so strong that I took my leave of Dagmar abruptly.

She said to me: "Until tomorrow."

That evening, I spoke thus to my grave soul, which disapproved of me:

"Why recoil before the certainty of a joy and perhaps a consolation? Hope is the only light thread that can guide us through the labyrinth—a tenuous thread, ready to break, but perhaps salvation. I could drink that blue water of the dawn. I could respire that bouquet of eglantines. I could see the dawn without terror and could sleep all night . . ."

At that moment, I received a letter from Lorely:

> *What an unstable thing your heart is! I be-*
> *lieved that you had finally glimpsed me, that we*
> *could follow our common path in security and*

confidence. Raise your eyes, see better, contemplate me as I am. This dismal blindness cannot be, should not be. I tell you that it's impossible. I repeat it to you, with tears in the eyes. Oh, fear drying them up, those tears, of rendering me incapable even of weeping for you. In truth, every individual has to be similar to the appearance our obstinacy forms of them. Fear, by virtue of not comprehending me, rendering me incomprehensible, fear rendering me cruel by reproaching me for my cruelties, fear petrifying me by criticizing my indifference. A thought can do us so much harm, and what you think of me does me more harm than you imagine, and more than I know myself.

Can it be that everything is consummated? And are you only going to seek banal amours in future, in order to forget the passion to which you have sacrificed your entire existence?

What do you hope to gain by trampling gods broken by your hands? Their mutilated grace will haunt you forever. Your fake happiness will never equal the disgust you have for yourself.

When you have understood the error that separates us, come back to me . . .

All night long I waited feverishly for the approach of dawn. It came quickly, ugly and solemn, like a nativity, seemingly fearful of the unknown life. But what did the sadness of the dawn matter to me? Did I not have hope within me?

I dared not confess to myself the uncertain joy that was delighting me, in the fear of seeing it vanish. I dared not go to Dagmar's house, and it was not until the approach of sunset that I found the courage to go and knock on her door.

She was standing on the perron, her eyes hypnotized by the sumptuous sky.

"Look at those clouds!" she cried. "They're like three very pious and very powerful kings, who are bringing vases of gold and ciboria ornamented with precious stones in order to adorn altars."

"You are," I said, "a princess who sings and plays, in solitude, with her opal necklace. While waiting for the unknown prince, she goes to sleep every night to the sounds of an invisible harmony to which her little sisters, the fays, give birth all around her."

Dagmar, fingering her opals, stimulated their flames capriciously.

"Opals," she murmured. "Yes, I love them. I also like round turquoises." She smiled, the pretty smile of a perverse child.

Then I said to her: "You must have listened to innumerable confessions—whispered in twilight, murmured on evenings like this one, or sobbed in the darkness."

"I've had a great many lovers, yes."

"Of both sexes, Dagmar; for I've heard you sing:

> *For I would dance to make you smile, and sing*
> *Of those who with some sweet mad sin have played . . .*
> *And low Love walks with delicate feet afraid*
> *'Twixt maid and maid . . .* [1]

---

1 These lines are given in English in the original. They were addressed to Natalie Barney by Olive Custance (1874-1944), after Barney wrote her an admiring letter regarding her collection *Opals* (1901). Natalie

"You must have collected that song from the passionate lips of a lover . . ."

"I like the love of women and that of men," she confessed. "I don't share the grim exclusivism of women who, for the love of women, hate and scorn the love of men. But I prefer the incomparable tenderness of women to the rude vehemence of men more often than not."

I considered her. "Pretty poem in porcelain, what words are delicate enough to tell you my gratitude? I can see again, for having encountered on my route the dream in Saxe that you are."

She was still smiling, without responding. For a long time I contemplated her parted lips, like a wild rose.

"Would you like," she said, "to take me to see the fireworks that are being displayed tonight? I adore the ambitious rockets, the showers of stars and the broken rainbows . . ."

---

invited Custance to Paris, and suggested that she, Tarn and Custance form the basis of a community of female poets, like Sappho. Custance came—accompanied by her mother and by Freddy Manners-Sutton, who later became engaged to Barney—although she appears to have been infatuated with Lord Alfred Douglas, whom she married in 1902. Some commentators say that Tarn conceived an intense dislike for Custance; others say that she competed with Barney for her affections (both might be true). This was before Tarn was summoned to Nice to Violette Shillito's deathbed, and while Tarn went to Nice, Natalie went to Venice with Custance, whom she called "Opale." It might have been partly for that reason that Tarn refused to see Barney when she returned to Paris, and the two were still estranged when Natalie went to America in 1902, while Tarn moved to her new apartment in the Avenue du Bois and began her relationship with Hélène de Zuylen. Goujon suggests that Dagmar is based on Custance, presumably on the basis of the quotation and her liking for opals, although the character seems to bear no resemblance at all to the English poet, who was three years older than Tarn.

"I'll come to fetch you this evening, little princess."

The hour finally sounded. She took my arm. The contact of that slender body intoxicated me. The consciousness of my strength increased in my own eyes. I felt proud of having softened a being who dominates and protects. I loved the seductive child in Dagmar. Her childish perversity was one charm more, a charm of anxiety and disquiet.

. . . A comet launched forth vertiginously, rose up recklessly as far as the most distant constellations. Then there was a brief thunder, and a cascade of azure radiance.

"Oh," sighed Dagmar, "the snow of blue stars. Can you see them? Can you see them?"

She addressed me as *tu*, as a child would to a little comrade. She did not even know what she was saying, entirely given to the ecstasy of those shooting stars, green, white and red.

"How beautiful it is," she murmured, "that lightning before the stars. One moment, the whole sky is as white as the Milky Way! Now it's streaming with the heroic blood of giants . . . Oh, it's decorated with crimson, it's like a vast carpet of violets . . . No, no, it's greener than the ocean on a spring evening. How beautiful it is, and how happy I am!"

Her eyelids fluttered, and her dazzled eyes sought mine in order to surprise the reflection of her joy there. I laughed like her, I laughed with her laughter. In truth, we had the souls of two infants . . .

But when the last rocket went out, my gaiety fell with it. We went back via an avenue of centenarian oaks.

"I'm almost afraid of these trees," said Dagmar, shivering. "They're higher than the vault of a Gothic cathedral. I'd be afraid, I'd be very afraid, if you weren't here . . ."

She huddled against me, with a chilly gesture. I would have liked to carry her far away, to lie her down on a narrow bed as soft as a cradle and cover her fragile bare feet with kisses.

"Aren't you tired, Dagmar?"

"Yes . . . I've looked at the rockets so much that I finally feel weary . . ."

The luminous laughter of her eyes belied her words. We sat down on a marble bench.

I drew closer to Dagmar.

"Pretty, oh, too pretty, why have I so much anguish in loving you?"

She was only slightly astonished, and not offended.

"Tell me again, and better, that you love me," she commanded, imperiously.

"O my lover of the dawn! If you knew with what soft tenderness I surround you! It's very simple, but I would weave it in a thousand phrases, in order that it would appear eternally new to you. I want to render it versatile and changing, like the opals and the rainbows that you prefer . . ."

She inclined her forehead on my shoulder.

"I love you, Dagmar, with such an indulgent caress of the soul that your future treasons will never waken the slightest anger in me. And yet, if I loved you later with a passion like the one that ravaged me . . . who knows?"

XXXVI

WE were in Dagmar's garden.

"You're more eglantine than ever," I murmured. "I've never seen freshness comparable to yours."

And the sudden thought came to me that it would be unexpected and sweet to forget, next to that adolescence, my long tortures. For Dagmar it would be the caprice of an hour of ennui, and for me, the unhoped-for consolation.

But an anxiety retained me. Would I dare to put my excessively heavy heart in the hands of a child?

"What are you thinking about," the little princess asked me. "Your thoughts always make me anxious."

I looked into the depths of her blue eyes at all the springtime that was reflected there.

"If you want to put your unsuspicious hand of a little girl in mine, Dagmar, I'll respire next to you the air of the dawn."

Her exceedingly clear eyes did not flinch under my gaze. And in her perverse candor, she extended her lips to me.

"Have you no fear, Dagmar?"

My voice tore the invisible veils that the silence had just woven around us.

"Of what could I be afraid?"

"My love."

"Is it necessary to fear love?" she asked, so ingenuously that I recoiled before the kiss that she was offering me. I recoiled as an individual that dementia has struck, taking a step back before the murder conceived in an insensate hour.

And I said:

"There is still space in me for pity becoming tender before weakness—exquisite confident weakness. You won't suffer from your puerile curiosity, Dagmar."

XXXVII

THE magical little princess went away for long days. I thought about her as one smiles at ancient childhoods . . .

Toward the end of a rainy afternoon, I was lingering in the library when the door opened. Dagmar advanced toward me, hesitantly.

"I've come to give you some very serious news," she said, in a vaguely hasty voice. "But first let me warm myself up and dry my soaking dress a little."

I lit a capricious fire for her. The flames made her bright eyes shine.

"Give me a cigarette."

From her childishly greedy lips, a smoke was exhaled more subtle than an opium dream.

"Dusk," she said, "is like a woman weeping alone in a silent room, where white flowers are wilting. The petals fall silently, one after another, and the moment is quivering with shameful dreams. In the distance, memories pass by in floating tunics. Stars shine at their sandals . . ."

"You're a poet, like Eranna of Telos, the virgin loved by Psappha who died at nineteen. But what's the grave news that you mentioned just now?"

She blushed faintly.

"You've told me that I was a little princess waiting on the terrace for the arrival of the husband . . ."

There was an anxious silence.

"The prince for whom I was waiting has come to me . . ."

A delicate Saxe shepherdess, who resembled Dagmar, was playing mute music on porcelain pipes. Dolorously, I picked up the excessively pretty and excessively frail ornament, and broke it.

Dagmar extended her imploring hands toward me.

"Spare me your rancor. I hardly merit it."

"There's no rancor in me, only melancholy. I'm not blaming you, Dagmar, I'm weeping for you . . ."

"I tremble for my happiness," she said, shivering. "Society is like a dragon that never falls asleep, the cruel dragon of tales of enchantment. Oh, who will defend us against the hatred of the world? We're two children, he and I, lost in the dark forest."

The rain was falling outside, isolating our anxieties like a drawn curtain, separating us from the world and people. It made a noise like the silk of long trains.

"I don't know why," I said, in order to veil with speech the torment of my soul, "the rain reminds me of distant waves."

"Waves . . ." murmured Dagmar. "I seem to see tides casting silver and glaucous flowers toward us."

"Dagmar," I sobbed, "can it be that our routes will be separated forever?"

Slowly, she stood up.

"My life is different from yours. Cloistered behind a hawthorn hedge, I scarcely divine the menacing ugliness of society. I don't know human existence. I don't know the passions and anguish reflected in your sore . . . your wicked . . . eyes . . ."

"In truth, Dagmar you haven't known human existence. That's why I haven't dared to love you."

She turned away, and pensively, said: "Adieu," in a whisper.

"Adieu, Dagmar . . ."

As she went, she brushed the broken statuette with her Kate Greenaway dress with long pleats.

XXXVIII

THE torment of April was finally extinct. The summer, dear to Our Lady of Fevers, surged forth from the burning earth. The image of Lorely reigned implacably over the torrid hours . . .

I dreaded flowers, as sly adversaries; I dreaded music, as a perfidious enemy; for flowers and music conceal all the treasons of memory. The voluptuous angers of old were tearing me apart, like as many charming monsters . . .

Sometimes, teeth clenched for a mute defense, I struggled against the force that drew me toward Lorely . . .

One day, however, I awoke with a less heavy soul. It seemed to me that perfumes of violets had bathed my forehead while I slept. The oppression that stifled me when I awoke had disappeared. I no longer feared the sunlight coming in through the open window or the odor of honeysuckle that rose from the garden.

I asked myself very quietly what unknown sweetness had thus dissipated the pestilential breath of Our Lady of Fevers. And, looking outside, I perceived that summer had just fled before autumn.

For a long time, I wandered by the water into which the russet tresses of willows were dipping. The appeasement of faded flowers infiltrated into me.

With an uncertain expectation. I raised my eyes. In front of me, serene in the serenity of October, I saw Eva.

She seemed the very incarnation of autumn. In her long hands, or martyrs, chrysanthemums were expiring, mingled with dead leaves. The melancholy pleats of her dress fell around her. She was mounted in stained glass windows more splendid than the rainbow and the sunset . . .

I thought that once, in an excessively noisy city, I had murmured her mystical name. And suddenly, the ringing of aerial bells had floated above the tumult of the discordant streets. The pious carillon sang her name, proclaimed it, cast it to the winds:

"Eva! Eva! Eva!"

She approached. No speech broke the charm of the mystery.

"My sweet Autumn, my dear Autumn," I stammered, finally.

I thought that she and I were standing on the threshold of eternity. The invisible stained glass threw around her a glory so miraculous that I could not sustain its glare. A hope as vast as the sadness rose up in my heart.

She only replied to me with her grave smile.

I don't know why the image of Dagmar, that poem in porcelain, loomed up between us with its disquieting charm of fragility.

An anguish more terrible than any human anguish gripped me at that moment. My eyes were attached to Eva's eyes, distant and gray, as if seen through clouds of incense.

I repeated the words of yesterday: "Aren't you afraid, Eva?"

"I fear nothing," she said.

It was a murmur on an organ in the depths of crepuscular chapels.

"Will you be stronger than my sickness?" I implored.

"I shall be stronger than all human woes, since I am pity."

There was a religious silence around us. I dared not sob to her: "I love you!"

XXXIX

A year later, the summer evening, white with clematis, brought us together again in the library, where one respired a charming odor of faded flowers and old wood. On the mantelpiece, next to the portrait of Ione, white violets were leaning.

Eva said to me in a low voice: "The moment is very grave. From the unknown, entering through the open window . . ."

Suddenly, I respired a strange perfume, more subtle than the perfume of flowers, which was exhaled from the garden, and rose toward me. I shuddered, as if at the approach of an indeterminate peril.

"I'll reveal to you now, since it's necessary, what I've hidden from you until now, fearing for the health of your sick soul . . ."

Eva stopped, her eyelids divinely thoughtful, before murmuring: "Lorely has returned . . ."

She waited. I understood the immense significance of those few simple words. Lorely had expelled from her presence the man whom she had never loved. She was weary of the infamous comedy. She had become herself again, the inviolable priestess of neglected altars . . .

I could go to Lorely, begging her to forgive me for all the harm she had done me and I had done to myself for her. I could revive the exquisite sufferings, of which I retained the incurable imprint.

It seemed to me that I was reborn in the flame that had once consumed my dolorous flesh. I regretted the past bitterness even more than the acute and brief joys.

"Lorely," I stammered. "Lorely . . ."

The splendor disappeared, and my eyes encountered once again the mystically clouded eyes of Eva. They had the sadness that is dormant in the eyes of saints impotent to soothe the dolors kneeling before them.

"The mirage has dissipated, Eva."

She stood up, diaphanous in the semi-darkness.

"I'll leave you to your two former councilors, silence and solitude."

"Aren't you my silence, Eva? Aren't you my solitude?"

Slowly, and with infinite gentleness, she disengaged her hands from mine, which were trying to hold her back, and disappeared into the depths of the dusk, which enveloped her like a veil . . .

Gradually, the darkness was illuminated by an equivocal smile. It was Lorely, the flower of Selene, the eternal feminine temptation. An ambiguous cruelty sharpened the steely gleam of her gaze. I believed that those two women were the two archangels of destiny: Lorely, the perverse archangel; Eva, the redemptive archangel; Lorely, perfumed with poisons, adorned with aconite and belladonna; Eva, bearing on her forehead the red aureole of a martyr, shredding expiatory lilies under her feet.

I pronounced aloud, invoking I know not what invisible presences: "Choose . . ."

"Never choose," interjected an androgynous voice that responded to my hesitation. "One always regrets what one has not chosen."

"My sweet San Giovanni, what do you advise me to do in this indecisive hour?"

The Annunciatrix smiled strangely; the evening smiles thus at its image reflected in the water.

"It's necessary to prefer violence to tenderness and passion to amour," she said. "It's cowardly to esteem happiness more highly than radiant suffering."

"I'm neither a salamander nor a phoenix, and I can't live in that which destroys and consumes."

"So much the worse for you; you'll never be a poet. No poet has ever been happy. No one is, in any case, a poet or a saint while alive. But you won't be a poet in death, since you haven't been able to love."

"I've loved to the limit of my strength," I said, defending myself. "No one has the right to ask any more of a human being. Later, I was exhausted and I renounced the vain struggle. Like Dante, I've wandered in the stormy night, and I've knocked on the door of the monastery, imploring peace. A nun opened up to me the sanctuary in which my soul was divinely consoled."

"No word of wisdom is worth as much as the laughter of a fool," said the Annunciatrix.

She continued:

"It's necessary never to retain resentment against a woman. The injustices of women and their angers are like the injustices and angers of the gods. It's necessary to accept them with love and submit to them with resignation. And certainly, no individual is culpable for not loving another. That is why Lorely has never committed the slightest sin in your regard."

She went on, even more quietly:

"Listen to the counsel of music. Listen to the counsel of flowers, since the only oracles that remain to you are songs and perfumes. Music will bring you back to your pagan priestess by virtue of the magic of dream. Flowers will bring you back to her by means of the prestige of memory . . ."

She disappeared, and I remained in my troubled solitude. Stars were singing in the profundity of space.

The strange perfume, more imperious than ever, attracted me like an appeal. I stood up and frayed a passage for myself through the nocturnal foliage.

XL

THE silence was terrible by virtue of its intensity: a silence of anguish that enfevered the night. The plants were vaguely fearful of the words that we were about to pronounce, and the trees were thoughtful, like grave prophets saddened by the future . . .

Lorely, her hair more fluidly green and her eyes bluer than the moon, was waiting. Her frail silhouette stood out against the blue-tinted grass, framed by the glaucous foliage. Momentarily, I contemplated the form and visage of my past.

"Lorely . . ."

She did not raise her eyes. She was like the statue of a dead woman.

"Lorely . . ."

Finally, the pallor of that apparition became animated.

"I've come to you to take you back. You belong to me, for I am your first love. You belong to me, above all, because I was the first to make you suffer. I am your destiny. You can flee me, but you can never forget me."

"I shall never forget you, Lorely. I would never want to forget you."

A victorious gleam traversed Lorely's lunar eyes.

"I knew that, and that's why I've come to you."

As before, I feared her cruel smile.

"You haven't been able to conquer me," Lorely pronounced, slowly. "You haven't had the strength, the patience or the courage to vanquish my hostile withdrawal from any individual who wants to dominate me."

"I'm not unaware of that, Lorely. I'm not formulating the slightest reproach, the slightest complaint. I retain an inexpressible gratitude to you for having inspired in me the amour that I wasn't able to make you share."

"I said to you once: 'Only love me just enough to illuminate my existence.'"

"And I wasn't wise enough to obey you."

She was carrying orchids as avid as unassuaged lips. She detached them and shredded them one by one with her long, implacable fingers.

"It was necessary to feel sorry for me for being incapable of a unique and sincere passion," she said, "for I know nothing sadder in the world than wandering perpetually, wandering in quest of an inaccessible tenderness."

Eros has made me love without closing my eyes.

"Oh, Lorely!" I sighed.

She went on:

"I have more need of you than I would have believed, and differently. I have need of you . . ."

The tobacco flowers were paling in the shadow. Their nocturnal perfumes put my reason and my conscience to sleep. They triumphed over everything that was not as subtle, perilous and perfidious as themselves.

D'antico amor senti la gran Potenza . . .[1]

"One belongs to one's past," Lorely emphasized. "Everything down here would be too facile if one could escape the consequences of one's actions. I am your past and you belong to me."

"One belongs to one's future. I belong to my future . . . and to Eva."

"The past is truer than the future. The future is uncertainty, the past is written in ineffaceable letters."

Lorely's voice was sovereignly imposing. I replied to her with an evasive remark.

"I said to Eva this very morning: '*I would like to spread throughout the universe a little of the joy that comes to me from your presence.*'"

"What joy can equal dolor? Dolor is stronger than joy. One can forget a joy, one never forgets a dolor. I am your suffering, that is why you will never cease to love me. Suffering alone is true, and happiness is not."

"I have the certainty that happiness is tangible, that it is as true as the dream," I replied. "But it is necessary to struggle even more bitterly to keep it than to conquer it."

"I covet a higher ideal for you than happiness. I want you to be free, in order that nothing diminishes you by absorbing you. I want you to be free, in order that you can contemplate what is above you. You are so weak when you love, even if only slightly and confusedly, as you loved me. And I fear for us the harm that might be done to you."

I listened with troubled astonishment to the new gravity in her voice.

1 "The great power of ancient amour" (Dante perceiving Beatrice in canto XXX of the *Purgatorio*).

"I am thinking," she said, "of the passage of the giant. The future is similar to a mountain road that it is necessary to hollow out in the rock. The crowd stops. Hesitant and stupid, before the insurmountable blocks, but a giant lifts them up and marches on. He frays a heroic passage through the brambles and the stone. Thirst consumes him and solitude enfevers him. He perishes before reaching the other slope. Then the irresistible force of all those weaknesses runs along the road that he has traced. They are seen to swarm in millions where the precursor giant died. If there is truly something great in you, do as he did; go toward your destiny. Disdain cowardly happiness; choose the better part, which is that of tears."

"I don't know whether happiness, infinitely rare, is inferior to suffering, the universal lot," I protested.

"Let's be calm and limpid, shall we? Let's not plunge thus into the depths of verity and lies. The night seems weary to me—as weary as me. But tomorrow, I shall be reborn with the dawn, and I will be April or you, with indecisive laughter, April, whose joy conceals promises of sad harvests, crops still dormant."

"There can be no dawn in the past, Lorely. The past dies with the last stars. Only the future is the dawn."

"I'm sick of reason and verity. I'm sick of everything that is not simple amour."

I replied:

"Amour also has its hopeful dawns, its fervent middays, its melancholy sunsets and its long moonless nights. You know that better than I do, you who fear metamorphosis more than death."

Lorely turned away, obliquely.

"I had in my soul an entire heritage of spring. Open your arms and your heart to me again. I won't reawaken any anguish in you. I won't bring you any vestige of a past that isn't ours. Piously, like those who enter a temple, I shall enter your heart, and if I find a joy there that is faded by being already old, I'll replace it with a freshly blossomed joy. I have a soul full of flowers . . ."

"If you're inclining toward me, Lorely, it's only because I escaped you like a danger. I loved you too much not to fear you eternally. I've lost hope and confidence since . . . since you! But a savior has come to me . . ."

"You're stubborn in only seeing ugly and sad things in our past. Remember the lilies!"

The sky was like a marvelous ceiling of cedar, nacre and ivory, and the trees loomed up, as svelte and white as Moorish columns. The night seemed a palace of Boabdil, meditating in a dream of the past.

"I remember, Lorely."

She stopped and said: "Amour is a Calvary where roses flourish."

A dead serpent lay at our feet. An oblique ray of moonlight made the green scales glitter strangely, which appeared to quiver with a slow undulation. And I remembered a few enigmatic phrases:

> *Dead serpents revive under the gaze of those who love them. The magical eyes of Liliths reanimate them, as moonlight reanimates stagnant waters . . . Dead serpents insinuate themselves through the darkness, where their eyes dart gleams. For, being faithful, they serve the Liliths and lie in wait for the prey that they have designated to them.*

. . . Our Lady of Fevers was corrupting the garden with her mortal breath. The foxgloves and the belladonnas extended their perfumes and their poisons toward her. The reptiles crawled all the way to her paludal reliquary and brought her as an offering their venomous souls. A lunar leprosy corroded the trees, and the red roses bled like livid wounds. I wanted to flee the pestiferous garden, but I could not take my eyes off Lorely, her hair greener and her eyes bluer than nocturnal gleams.

"Remember the lilies," she said.

A distant lamp cast a glow over the violent shadow in which the tobacco flowers were dying. That glow was as consoling as the calm reflection of a star.

Then it disappeared.

Lorely's blonde morbidity attenuated further under the moon.

"A dolor sharper than joy, a joy more profound than dolor," she emphasized. "All the passion that peace scorns . . ."

Again the lamp cast a starry radiance. It was vacillating in Eva's hands; she was approaching us.

In truth, those two women were the archangels of destiny: Lorely, clad in green, Eva, clad in violet, both strangely luminous.

"This is the hour of the soul," Eva murmured.

Between the three of us, there was a pause. What I was about to say was decisive and fatal. All the terror of the choice weighed upon me.

When the final word was pronounced, a sigh rose from the penumbra.

"Adieu . . . and *au revoir* . . ."

A WOMAN
APPEARED TO ME

(1904)

The Charmer of Serpents, to whom serpents had taught their tenebrous wisdom, spoke thus to the ephebe:

"Happiness is as vast and noble as despair. It is necessary that happiness frightens, like despair.

"The only true happiness is that of the hermit and the solitary. It is necessary that happiness, like despair, should be indifferent to all people and to their words and thought.

"I have only one example to propose, the example of the Woman in the ermine mantle. When her ermine mantle came unfastened and fell miserably in the mud, passers-by picked it up and held it out to her; but, with a haughty gesture, she turned away and went on her way, shoulders bare under the wind and the rain.

"Refrain from moderation as others refrain from excess. For Prudence is the sole dangerous adversary of heroism and happiness.

"Never follow advice, even one of those that I give you. Every individual ought to live their personal life and pay dearly for the experience that proves nothing.

"The sole dolor without stars is that of people who suffer from not suffering.

"Amity is more perilous than amour, for its roots are stronger and deeper than the roots of amour.

"The dolor of amity is more bitter than the dolor of amour.

"Certain people love amity as others love amour. They suffer by virtue of amity as others do by virtue of amour. They only have one amity in their existence, as others only have one amour. It is at the moment when amity escapes them that they finally despair.

"And it is when they finally despair that they encounter their happiness.

"For happiness is like the magnificence of ruins.

"This is what the serpents, counselors of sensuality, have taught me:

"Flee the act of initiation, as cowardly as pillage, as brutal as rape, as bloody as massacre, and only worthy of a drunken and barbaric soldier.

"If the woman you love is a virgin, leave to a stranger the violation of her first modesties. Amour ought to be pure of everything that is not sensuality. Suffering in amour is discordance in music.

"Do not fear the nocturnal breath of flowers beside your slumber.

"For their perfumes appease the invisible Presences.

"Fear slumber, which brings dreams heavy with fear, and the anguish that makes one bless the dawn, the gray awakening itself.

"But do not fear Death.

"For the Dead, lying on a bed of violets, finally find the dreams that existence has not animated, the vanished perfumes and the extinct music.

"For the Dead alone find, intact and pure of any cruel memory, the amity that once deceived and the amour that once betrayed."

San Giovanni.

I
[Chopin. Op. 44.]

"*COME this evening . . . I am avid for stars,*" I wrote in haste. Vally's pupils seemed to be contemplating me ironically through the blue orchids with falling clusters. I joined to that short note the large winter flowers that she loves, the flowers of art that cannot blossom freely in the air and sunlight.

I went out under the crepuscular rain, and intoxicated myself mortally on the marvelous sadness of the drizzle. I bore a feverish melancholy in my heart.

"Vally," I murmured through the mist. "Vally." Her name returned to my lips like a sob.

I evoked the already distant hour when I saw her for the first time, and the frisson that ran through me when my eyes encountered her eyes as sharp and blue as a blade. I had the obscure prescience that that woman would intimate the order of destiny to me, and that her face was the redoubtable face of my Future. Near her I felt the luminous vertigoes that rise from the abyss, and the appeal of very deep water. The charm of peril emanated from her and attracted me inexorably.

I did not try to flee, for I would have escaped death more easily. We departed together toward the Wood of winter evenings. My eyes were dazzled by the snow. All that light seemed florid with unreal espousals. Around us and within us there was a nuptial chastity, a white sensuality.

I spoke to her very quietly, in a voice weakened by all the fears of first love:

"You are not like the One of whom I dreamed, and yet I find in you the incarnation of my most distant desires. You are less beautiful and stranger than my dream. I love you but I already have the certainty that you will never love me. You are the suffering that enables the scorn of happiness. I saw you today for the first time, and I am the shadow of your shadow.

"How those moonstones please me, those moonstones that are weeping their tears of light on your breast! Through the pleats of the silver fabric, I divine the naked beauty of your body. Everything that you have impregnated with your enigmatic grace enchants me. I adore your mysterious and pale tresses.

"I will be what you make of me. For you are the marvelous Priestess of a symbol I do not know."

"I love your amour," Vally murmured. "I'm afraid of understanding you and I tremble at attracting you irremediably. My illusions are poor clowns that grimace at one another through their tears. I would like so much to love you, to love you in my moments of silence, which would finally be eternalized! Do you not see how I weep my joys and how I laugh my sadness? I would like so much to love you," her pale lips repeated.

"My amour is great enough to remain solitary," I replied. "I love you, and that is sufficient for my ecstasy and my sobs. You will never love me, Vally, for you have within you such an ardor to live and feel that the passion of all individuals will not content you."

I traversed two weeks of fearful amazement with Vally.

I experienced the stupor of an acolyte intoxicated by sacred perfumes. I glimpsed everything through fumes of incense and aromatics. My strange felicity left a mystic astonishment in my soul. Later, I understood that those hours were the Unforgettable Hours of memories and regrets.

When studious lassitudes overwhelmed me, my Loreley slowly and gently dropped rose petals on my eyelids. When I suffered her silent refusals, she brought me black irises and Palestinian arums, lilies of darkness opened under the gaze of perverse archangels. I contemplated, in a glad anguish, her mouth with the Florentine smile and her eyes of mortal blue, but I preferred the moonlight of her vague tresses.

As I drew away from her abode, I turned round to see her on her balcony, haloed with azure and chimerically distant.

"I smile at everything that weeps and I weep before everything that smiles," she said.

Thus, her enigmatic soul was veiled under paradoxical remarks that only revealed her partially.

Her methodical cruelty sometimes extracted a plaint or a semblance of reproach from me. Vally posed her icy eyes upon me.

"It's me for whom it's necessary to feel sorry, and you that it's necessary to envy. Since you have been able to discover the amour for which I have been searching in vain for so many wasted years, reveal it to me. I would like so much to love you," she said again, like a dolorous refrain of her lips weary of my lips.

Sometimes, she allowed me to glimpse the hope of perhaps attaining her one day.

"You will understand later the negligibility of the pleasures for which I neglect you. And you will only see then, in the avidity with which I search for them, my fear of seeing them vanish."

I wanted to tame for her sake my violent tyrannies, my awkwardly passionate jealousies. Vally criticized me for demanding a Christian fidelity, against which her instincts of a young Fauness revolted. Her pagan joy burst forth in multiple amours. She had for symbols the variable April, the rainbow and the opal, everything that shines and changes in accordance with the momentary reflection.

"The one who gives has the right to ask in exchange," I said to her, in the times when I still hoped to retain her fugitive soul. "I give you a loyally unique amour; may I not ask in return for an equal constancy?"

But I soon fathomed the abyss of my folly . . .

"Like Art," she replied, "amour is complex, and it is necessary, in order finally to possess it, to follow a difficult route for a long time.

"The artist who dreams a statue does not seek his divine vision in a unique model. He finds absolute splendor through dissimilar individuals, each of whom reveals to him what they have of the most beautiful. And for my passionate dream, it is necessary for me to combine scattered perfections, in order to confound them in a harmonious ensemble created by my dreams. What I love in you is your power of amour, slightly savage, slightly primitive, but absolute."

"You're frightfully right, Vally. You're April. Only these lines of Swinburne can express and contain you entirely: '*A mind of many colors, and a mouth/Of many tunes and kisses.*' As for me, I love you dolorously, like all simple individuals."

"You love me badly," my Flower of Selene interrupted. "You love me badly, since you can neither retain me nor comprehend me."

"One always loves badly, Vally. To love well is no longer to love amorously."

She considered me with a mild scorn.

"Can you not raise yourself all the way to magnificent disinterest? Amour is nothing but a perpetual self-immolation before an adored image. When I encounter in passing an apparition of grace and charm that delights me, you ought to rejoice in the felicity that a brief illusion accords me."

"I don't know whether I can raise myself as far as that grandeur of renunciation, Vally. For the road that leads to the summits of pure tenderness is more dolorous than the road of crucifixions."

"*I have dreamed of a Calvary where roses flourish*," quoted Vally, smiling palely.

"A beautiful thought in a beautiful verse, my perfidious Sweetness. So be it. I don't know, in any case, why I should have the stupid pretention to forbid you the varying infinity of the Feminine. As for me, is it my fault if, by virtue of an evident inferiority, I can't turn my desires and my dreams toward another Beauty? The embrace of my amour is tightened around a single individual, yours is as vast as that of mercy. You have the better part. Melancholy Christianity has, I fear darkened all my *joie de vivre* in binding me uniquely, in accordance with Indissoluble Marriage, to the person I love. Your conception of amour is vaster and more beautiful, mine is born of my obscure atavisms."

And we united our feverish lips in a kiss in which we could already taste the bitterness of future regrets.

II
[Warum. Schumann.]

I went into Vally's drawing room, my temples damp with drizzle. Tiger lilies opened their vast corollas from which the vehemence of perfumes was exhaled. Vally, languidly extended on a divan of Persian fabrics, was entertaining a few friends. Her white dress veiled her while revealing her. She excelled in the savant composition of such lascivious loose garments. Her undone hair formed a lunar aureole around her forehead.

Next to her, the scholar Petrus, a translator and commentator of Zoroaster, was pronouncing banal sentences that took on pornographic meanings, so libidinous was the expression of his fat lips. He bore a terrible resemblance to a merchant in a Levantine bazaar. His ample gestures seemed to be deploying excessively gaudy carpets before imaginary clients. His conversation, like his manner of writing, evoked sickening odors, barbaric colors and all the bad taste of an Orient of shoddy gods. He talked too much, doubtless in the hope of providing a counterpart to the silence of his wife, a novelist of fine tumultuous genius, who did not talk enough. Distant, she seemed lost in a perpetual dream. The floating pleats of her green dress streamed around her fluid body and made it resemble seaweed. A geranium stood out bloodily from her dark hair.

Slightly apart, Ione, the elected sister of my childhood was enfevered by a hallucinating thought. Her excessively broad and high forehead overwhelmed that pensive face. It hypnotized the gaze and almost made one forget the mysteriously sad brown eyes and the tender mouth.

Like Leonardo's equivocal San Giovanni, the Androgyne whose Italian smile illuminates the gallery of the Louvre so strangely, one of Vally's friends was listening to my Loreley develop her theory of Imitation in Art.

San Giovanni was a poet. Her verses were as perverse as her smile. Her renown did not extend beyond a very restricted circle of literate people and artists. On the other hand, her honest indecency scandalized the bourgeois and the artists alike. Only a few Iconoclasts venerated her for her audacity. Her volumes bore titles evocative of ambiguous sensualities: *Sur le Rhythme Saphique, Bona Dea* and *Les Mystères de Cérès Éleusine*.[1]

"The Imitator is almost always better endowed than the creator," said Vally, under the approving gaze of San Giovanni. "In the same way, the reflection is more beautiful than the color, and the echo sweeter than the sound. Shakespeare is the marvelous echo of Boccaccio, the echo of mountains that amplifies the voice and divinizes it in the prolongation to Infinity."

I spoke in a low voice, drawing closer to Ione:

"Don't think any longer, my excessively meditative Friend. Don't think any longer, I implore you in the name

---

1 The first title cited is a poem by Renée Vivien, the second a prose poem translated in *Lilith's Legacy*, and the third a slight variant of the title of another of her poems.

of our ancient tenderness. Love someone, love something. Amour is less perilous than thought. I know what hallucination is tormenting you. The Mystery of the inexplicable world haunts you perpetually. I've know those tortures before the Unknown. To escape the mortal obsession, I once created a theory of the Universe that at least had the merit of an extreme simplicity. I believe that the Unnamable, the Incomprehensible, is a double thought, a hermaphrodite thought. Everything that is ugly, unjust, ferocious and cowardly emanates from the Male Principle. Everything that is dolorously beautiful emanates from the Female Principle.

"The two Principles are equally powerful, and hate one another with an inextinguishable hatred. One will end up exterminating the other, but which will carry off the final victory? That enigma is the perpetual anguish of souls. We hope in silence for the definitive triumph of the Female Principle, which is to say the Good and the Beautiful, over the Male Principle, which is to say, over Bestial Force and Cruelty."

Ione was staring at her long hands, the color of old ivory. It was an unhealthy habit of hers to contemplate her hands for hours. She smiled without responding to me. Oh, the sadness of Ione's smile, more anguishing than the most bitter tears!

San Giovanni's voice recalled me abruptly to reality. She was defending her dearest theories against Petrus, who, blinking his libertine eyes, was discussing Alcaeus' verses to Psappha: *Weaver of violets, chaste Psappha with the honeyed smile, words rise to my lips but modesty restrains me.*

"Why chaste?" he interrogated. "The immortal Lover was nothing less than she was chaste."

"I pity you," the Androgyne interrupted, "for being unable to imagine an amour both ardent and pure, like a white flame. Such was the one that Psappha once devoted to her melodious Lovers. Is not that amour, evocative of Beauty in everything that it has of the most suave and delicate, a thousand times more chaste than the claustral solitudes in which obscene dreams and monstrous desires are exasperated? Is it not a thousand times more chaste than the cohabitation founded on interest that Christian marriage has become? Can one dream of anything more radiantly chaste than that school of virgins founded by a virgin, the school of Mytilene in which Psappha taught the complex arts of music and verse. In a time when only courtesans cultivated beautiful harmonies piously, that child of noble birth dared to consecrate herself entirely to the divine cult of Song."

"Psappha was certainly the great Unknown and the great Calumniated," mused Vally. "Has that virgin and that hereditary aristocrat not been confused with a vulgar courtesan? Has the legend not been invented of an infatuation with the fop Phaon, the stupidity of which is only equaled by its lack of historical veracity? And finally, has not the hypothesis been adopted universally of a marriage that the comic authors of Athens invented in order to ridicule her?"

"That pretended husband," added San Giovanni, supportively, "according to Suidas, quit the isle of Andros in quest of a wife. But the name of the husband, Kerkolas, plume-bearer, and that of his homeland, are sufficient indication of the kind of abject joke that gave birth to them. It was not, in any case, the custom of the Greeks to quit their city with the intention of marrying a foreigner."

"Only a vulgar soul could have substituted for the divine smile of Atthis and Eranna the bearded profiles of Kerkolas and Phaon," I approved.

"Base bourgeois morality has also taken possession of a fragment of Psappha: 'I posses a beautiful child whose form is like a golden flower, the beloved Kleis, whom I prefer to all Lydia and the lovable . . .' in order to transform the amorous slave Kleis into a legitimate daughter!"

San Giovanni paused, palely wrathful.

"That hideous image of bestial maternity after the *Ode to Aphrodita* and the *Ode to a Beloved Woman*!"

"Even her divine name has been travestied, the sonorous and sweet name of Psappha, for which the colorless appellation of Sappho has been substituted," Vally sighed. "Sappho! That suggests imperiously the mediocre statues and hackneyed verses by means of which the bourgeois crowd perpetuates the greatest feminine image that ever dazzled the World."

"How I love you in your mystical anger, my Priestess!" I murmured, very softly. "You appear to me then transfigured and almost supernatural."

Petrus would not let go. Now he was praising masculine beauty, superior, he affirmed, to feminine beauty.

"What is frightful," San Giovanni said to me, in a low voice, "is that I'm convinced that that man has the soul and the mores of the most honest bourgeois, and yet he gives the impression, at this moment, of a shady pimp offering English tourists the virginities of little boys. He's involuntarily obscene, like all Levantines. After his departure, one experiences the need to open the windows and shake the curtains."

"Adolescent boys are only beautiful because they resemble women," replied Vally, "and are still inferior to women because they have neither the graceful attitude nor the harmonious contours."

"Personally," San Giovanni meditated, "I believe that no statue of a young god surpasses the winged magnificence of the Victory of Samothrace, the supreme incarnation of feminine Beauty. I have a horror of Hercules. A Herakles," she emphasized, "is the apotheosis of the fairground wrestler and the apprentice butcher. I've never been able to absorb myself in the contemplation of tendons and musculature."

She collected herself, smiling.

"If it's true," she continued, "that the soul puts on several human appearances, I was once born in Lesbos. I was only a paltry child devoid of grace, when a companion older than me took me into the temple where Psappha was invoking the goddess. I heard the *Ode to Aphrodita*. The incomparable voice flowed, more harmonious than the sea. The verses unfurled like waves, and died and were reborn with a sound of tides. In truth, I once heard the *Ode to Aphrodita*. The melodious memory did not pale over the years, or through the centuries. However, I was only a taciturn child, and Psappha didn't love me. I loved her, and later, when I possessed feminine bodies, my sobs of desire went toward her. I was in Sicily when I learned of her death, but that death was so glorious that I didn't weep, and my companions' sobs surprised me and offended me. I reminded them of her magnanimous words: '. . . For it is not just that lamentations should be in the house of servants of the Muses; that is unworthy of us.'"

"Personally," mused the smiling Vally, "I was a little Arab shepherd boy. I slept all day and only woke up at the approach of the green or violet night. Toward evening, following my flock, I returned from the mountain and I walked in the midst of a great red dust. Out there, I was the first to see the rising moon. I ran all the way to the nearest village, proclaiming the moonrise. And all those to whom I announced the great news looked at the sky and rejoiced in seeing on the horizon the amber light that precedes the moon."

Petrus was meditative. His entire, slightly obese person expressed the meditation of a pacha digesting.

"Why do you hate men?" he finally asked San Giovanni, fixing his heavy eyes on her.

"I neither hate them nor detest them," San Giovanni replied, in a conciliatory fashion. "I hold it against them that they have done a great deal of harm to women. They are political adversaries that it pleases me to insult for the needs of the cause. Outside of the battlefield of Ideas, they're unknown and indifferent to me."

Petrus gave his oily face a solemn expression. One might have thought him a fakir gestating a prophecy. He contemplated the Androgyne for a long time before enunciating, in a fatal tone: "Mademoiselle, you are attempting in vain to escape the irresistible masculine seduction. You will certainly terminate your amorous career in the arms of a man."

The innocent conceit of his smile would have softened a Penthesilea, but anger bloodied the face of the poet of *Eleusinian Ceres*.

I stopped the words that were about to spring from her violent lips and I replied, in a profoundly shocked tone: "That would be an antiphysical aberration, Monsieur. I esteem our friend too much to believe her capable of an abnormal passion."

III
[Lied Ohne Ende. Schumann.]

GRADUALLY, the days softened as far as the warmth of spring. The April that Vally preferred allowed her bizarre smiles and enigmatic tears to be glimpsed. The fleeting hours united our dissimilar souls more narrowly. With time, my dolorous amour was affirmed and deepened.

She had an instinctive worship of the artificial. She loved to powder her pallor with pink. The false redness of her cheeks then contrasted in a disconcerting fashion with the attenuated light of her hair. Her mother, an Israelite, had transmitted to her the disconcerting charm of blonde Jewesses. Her eyes, more coldly blue than winter mists, distilled an Oriental gaze, a gaze of sensuality and languor. And her sinuous lips were made for lying even more than for kissing. One might have thought them laboriously sculpted by a subtle hand. They were lips devoid of tenderness, lips to which all the artifices of speech had long been familiar.

Sometimes, she put on the costume of a Venetian page, a lunar green velvet costume that harmonized delicately with her morbid hair. Sometimes, too, she transformed herself into a Greek shepherd. The music of an invisible syrinx then rose up around her footfalls, and her eyes laughed at the nudity of faunesses. Like all nostalgic souls, she sought the miracle of strange garments that disguise minds as well as bodies and resuscitate, for an hour, the grace of a vanished epoch. She was the Androgyne, as vigorous as an ephebe and as undulating as a woman. I admired fervently her ardor of a Priestess devoted to the worship of abandoned altars. I loved her reviving the flames of ruined temples and garlanding deflowered statues with roses.

Time passed with the flux and reflux of hours as monotonous as the sound of waves.

Petrus and his wife no longer crossed the threshold of the little drawing room with reflections of iris.

"That man is repulsive to me, like rancid rose water," Vally declared. "The infinite attraction of his wife cannot persuade me to tolerate that Levantine's presence. What a pity to see that marvelous individual, that flower, that alga, alongside such a bazaar merchant!"

Ione only came rarely. I had a heart so simultaneously happy and unhappy that I no longer worried about her long silences, or the contractions of her excessively high and broad brow. She seemed to be living an interior life that no foreign thought dared to penetrate, an intense and terrible life that was slowly exhausting all her strength. The perpetual interrogation of her gaze was as disturbing as that of hallucinated individuals before the abyss that will swallow them.

And I did not see anything of that struggle of a soul with the Unknowable, more tragically vain than that of the Man with the Angel. I did not see anything and I did not understand anything, for I no longer belonged to anything but the torments of that first amour, in which my bewildered being was struggling.

However, I sometimes went to visit the silent Ione. I always found her clad in a dress with ample pleats. It was a dark red dress that, I don't know why, put me in mind of evenings in Florence. A pendant of hieratic design, composed of a pale ruby mounted in green gold and terminated by a bizarre pearl was, along with a ruby belt, the only jewelry that she liked to wear. I spent taciturn hours with her. I dared not talk to her about Vally. I was not apprehensive of the censure of that soul, whose purity was ennobled by a very broad comprehension; but I sensed that Ione's tenderness would be alarmed by my tortures, divined in spite of my reticence. She knew, like me and better than me, how sterile my impossible effort to conquer the indifferent heart of Vally—who did not love me and never would love me—would be. She was not unaware that I was exhausting myself in futile suffering, and that thought darkened further the sadness of her eyes, as ardently brown as an autumnal night.

The constraint that weighed upon our words determined a distancing of souls between us. We feared one another's gaze as one fears a confession, and we feared our silences as treasons. We were afraid of the truth, and were afraid above all of our former frankness.

I went to see her less frequently; then my visits almost ceased. She did not make me the slightest reproach. More distant than a distracted stranger, she seemed insensible to everything that was not her mystical terror before the incomprehensible. And yet, she had been the pure sister to whom I had once confided all my inexpressible dreams . . .

IV
[Chopin. Op. 9.]

A N April day was ending. Vally received a note in which an excessively delicate and vague handwriting snaked: a handwriting of mystical sensuality or sensual mysticism. In the corner of the piece of paper, as yellow as old parchment, hieroglyphics were entangled that were revealed, after long and patient study, to be modern initials.

Won't you and your slave come to see me today?

We waited for San Giovanni in a strange green boudoir, the furniture of which was disquieting in its disconcerting sinuosity. The most ambiguous Art Nouveau triumphed there; the only reminder of other times was a reproduction of Leonardo's San Giovanni. That reproduction, surrounded by an atmosphere of comprehension and respect, seemed to be the portrait, or rather the very soul, of the Sapphic poet.

A desiccated serpent wound around a vase in which black irises were fading.

With an amicable curiosity, Vally considered the tarnished scales in which the living gleams and the sparkle of broken gems were forever extinct.

"Don't consider Dead Serpents too long," pronounced the voice of San Giovanni. Her silent footfalls had been muffled by the deep carpet without breaking the thread of our reverie. "For Dead Serpents revive under the gaze of those who love them. The magical eyes of Lilith reanimate them, as moonlight reanimates stagnant water."

"I remember," insinuated my pagan Priestess, "a story that you told me once. Your words trembled through a phantasmal dusk with the frissons of a Beyond intoxicated by terrors. Tell us the tale of the Dead Serpents, San Giovanni."

In a solemn whisper, the poet evoked the vision that had been suggested to her by an evening in which unadmitted anguishes had shivered slyly.

"It's the story of an American adventurer lost in the mountains," she explained.

She began:

"I wandered for several days over the mountain. The rocks amused me because of their fantastic resemblances to faces and animals. Some were like crouching chimeras and others attentive Nixes. I also recognized sharks and whales, obelisks, crocodiles and women's rumps. There were also the torsos of tortured giants and nuns kneeling under large stone veils.

"I played with beautiful and malicious lizards. I loved them liked gemstones. And during the sunsets, I felt sad all the way to my soul. I'm always sad at nightfall. And sometimes, dawn chills me like a presentiment.

"Solitude rendered me thoughtful. I often sit down in the dark and the shadow of death. Then I think about everything we don't know.

"Inexplicable fears traverse me at certain times. If I knew what I feared, I wouldn't be afraid any longer. I no longer dare move. I retreat into myself, like children huddling under the bedclothes. The horror of the Unknown capsizes my thought. Then, for a very long time, I remain motionless, looking ahead of me without having the courage to turn my head to the right or the left. It's terrible to be afraid without knowing why.

"I've never done any harm to anyone. I loved a young woman very purely. Her eyes never creased, when she laughed ardently amid the foliage. Her dark eyes belied the joy on her lips. She's dead . . .

"Later, I took a mistress. I cherish lizards because they resemble her. She liked to sleep in broad daylight. She didn't fear anything. Although she was joyful, I never heard her sing. Nothing made her tremble. She soon took another lover. Since then, I've been wandering in the mountains.

"Toward the end of an insolently blue afternoon, I was surprised to run into a strange little hut partly hidden under creepers. A hermit had to be sheltering his frenzy for isolation there.

"It had been a long time since I'd perceived a human face. So I lifted up the mat that served as the door of that solitary cabin.

"I had never seen such a bizarre dwelling. The walls, made of planks, were covered in shriveled and dried skins of snakes in which a vague gleam of scales still persisted.

"Huddled in a corner, an old man was grimacing with surprise and terror.

"I recoiled, vaguely fearful, before that narrow face with hollow cheeks. The yellow eyes, almost devoid of

142

eyelids, were dilated like the pupils of owls, nocturnal pupils wounded by the light. The chin was exaggerated, immeasurably long. And the rude white hair stuck up, as if raised by perpetual fright.

"I begged him to pardon my importunity. The old man, hallucinating me with his fixed contemplation, made no response. Believing that I was dealing with a deaf person, I raised my voice.

"'There's no need to shout,' said my host.

"That was as alarming as the noise of a breaking sepulcher. I hesitated . . . but curiosity was stronger than discretion.

"'Come in,' he shouted suddenly.

"The silence was prolonged.

"'I don't have the habit of talking,' he finally growled, as if to excuse himself.

"I examined the sinister place in which I found myself, curiously.

"'Why are you looking at the walls?' howled the solitary. 'I don't want you to look at the walls.'

"'I see that you're a killer of snakes,' I hazarded, timidly.

"I was consternated by the unexpected effect produced by such banal words.

"The hermit straightened up. His teeth chattered. He appeared to be struggling with a fit of fever. The crises dissolved into infantile sobs.

"'And you?' he asked, in an abrupt tone. 'Have you killed serpents?'

"'I've killed one or two,' I murmured, with an increasing anxiety.

"The old man bounded to his feet and, seizing my hands violently, shook me like a fruit tree.

"'Oh, you poor, poor fellow! Why did you do that? Didn't you know, then, that *it was futile?*'

"His voice decreased, and the sentence finished in a fearful whisper.

"'Don't you know, then, that serpents don't die? Or rather, they come back to life, more terrible and more venomous. They *come back to life*, I tell you.'

"The sun had set. A blue twilight rendered the dark corners mysteriously redoubtable.

"The old man was shivering like a Chinaman sick with opium.

"'It's getting dark,' I said, in order to break the anguished silence.

"'It's the hour when they come back to life, the hermit murmured. 'It's necessary never to kill serpents. Look! Look! Can't you see them crawling over the walls?'

"I don't know whether the solitary's terror took possession imperiously of my eyes and my mind . . . I don't know whether it was an illusion of the blue twilight . . . but I saw the snakes slithering, the desiccated scales of which resumed the sparkle of jewels. I saw their vindictive eyes staring at us, following us with hostile and knavish gleams. I saw them uncoiling and coiling. In my turn, I shivered mortally.

"'Look at that green serpent over there,' the hermit groaned. 'It's the most beautiful of them all. It has the living color of grass. In the prairie, one walks over those serpents without even seeing them. I've never struck a serpent more beautiful . . . And that one, with redness of sand . . . and that one, veined like a pebble, one of those that sleep in the midst of shingle . . . and that one, again, of rusty copper . . . All the serpents of all lands, which

I wanted to kill. They insinuate themselves through the cracks in the damp planks. They slither into dark corners . . . Look . . . Look . . .'

"I sensed cold contacts and viscous enlacements along my legs.

"Intoxicated by horror, I seized the arms of the pitiful solitary violently.

"'Why do you stay here? Why don't you run far away from these nightmares, these fevers and these deliria?'

"With a convulsive hand, he wiped away the glacial sweat that was bathing his brow.

"'I tried to go away once. That was a long time ago. They followed me. When I turned round I saw them, in the grass or under the rocks. They were hanging down from the branches of trees. They were swimming in streams. I saw them in the depths of the running water, like eels. They fascinated me with their maleficent eyes. In truth, I'm convinced that the Devil is a serpent. And it's perhaps for that reason that serpents are accursed and sacred. It's necessary never to kill a serpent, you see. Those you have killed in the past come back to life like the others.'

"The darkness was unfurling outside. A ray of moonlight was multiplied by the silver scales.

"'Oh, they'll be malevolent tonight. They love the moon, because it's as cruel as they are. They love the insidious moon. They're happy, and that renders them terrible. Oh, they'll be very malevolent tonight!'

"Was it the wind rustling in the creepers? I heard a hissing. I swear to you that I heard a hissing . . .

"I bounded toward the opening that served as a door. I galloped like an enraged horse over the mountain. I was crazy. An epileptic drool soiled my foaming lips.

"A green dawn finally rose over the summits. The funereal voice of the hermit was still ringing in my ears:

"'Don't kill serpents. They don't die. Or rather, they come back to life, more venomous and more terrible.'"

Vally was silent. A vague incredulity clouded her smile.

"Do you believe that the gaze of Liliths really reanimates dead serpents?" I asked her, finally.

"I'm certain of it," San Giovanni affirmed. "In the house of the soul, they crawl along indecisive routes. Through the semi-darkness, their eyes dart cruel gleams. For they serve the Liliths faithfully. They spy on the prey that they have designated to them. The person they watch senses, with a tenebrous horror, their cold coils tightening round the heart."

Vally was examining a Magdalen with a gravely nuanced wooden robe and a face and hands of porcelain. It was one of those dolls, of a mystical and puerile grace, that Spaniards group like mute actresses in a crucifixion scene. With a disinterested impulse, she was praying over human dolor. An exaltation of sincere dolor spiritualized that passionate face.

"That Magdalen resuscitates for me all the luminous ardor of Seville," San Giovanni reminisced. "Oh, the quivering acuity of the atmosphere! I sense myself becoming transparent in the subtle intensity of living."

She smiled at a memory.

"In Seville," she went on, "I was struck by something strange and very symbolic.

"They had recently wanted, as you know, to unify the time throughout Spain, and they had chosen for that the time marked by Greenwich. The clock of the cathedral of

Seville, alone, persisted obstinately in being a quarter of an hour behind. It challenged the other clocks; it mocked them; it seemed to glory in being *behind the times*. What do you think of that story, which is no less striking for being true?"

"I don't think anything; true stories don't interest me," said Vally. "To get as far away from nature as possible is the veritable goal of Art."

"You're right," confessed San Giovanni. "The person who imitates is only the vulgar copyist of the real. Only the person who creates is a veritable artist. In painting, I only like psychic landscapes, the flowers of dream and faces that I shall never contemplate. To create is to innovate, to produce what has never been seen or heard in Nature. Nature is inimitable; Art is unimaginable."

"I'd like to understand you, San Giovanni," I said, interestedly. "You're the bizarre flower of an unknown sap. I put a stubborn reflection into clarifying the obscure causes of which you are the paradoxical effect."

San Giovanni mirrored herself in the past. Her eyes lost themselves there, like eyes searching for their distant image in a mysteriously deep spring.

"I'm astonished myself by my strange childhood," she said. "It was a solitary germination, a childhood apart from others, almost outside human society. When passersby admired me with stupid tenderness, I retreated into the depths of my instinctive scorn, as one curls up in the depths of an accumulated shadow. While my companions complaisantly collected adulations and caresses, I gazed at those intruders with eyes that had become malevolent, in which a little hatred was already ignited."

She paused, in order to give her words more convincing weight.

"During my earliest years, I didn't love anyone. The most stubbornly obtuse sympathies were disconcerted by that unconscious hostility.

"Before being able to read, I diverted myself with the complex personality of my hands. My ten fingers each had an individuality, a character, almost a soul. The affirmative and bellicose thumb isolated itself with a natural pride. The index finger meditated in a prophetic wisdom. The middle finger extended over its limited empire the bourgeois despotism of an opulent father. The fourth finger, longer than the index finger, launched forth with a feminine slenderness. As for the little finger, it incarnated changing rebellion and girlish fantasy. I made my fingers speak. I attributed an existence to them, traversed by variable events and grave decisions."

"Ione's fingers," I put in, "are like long religiously pale candles."

San Giovanni went on:

"Like almost all children, I was deceitful and cruel. I lied by virtue of the need for the impossible and the beyond. I spread in badly stitched inventions all the dreams that I had already accumulated over the years.

"I took pleasure in tormenting my younger comrades by telling them terrifying stories of specters. Their fear delighted me with an ingenuous intoxication. But I experienced even more from my own demonic imagination.

"No perverse dream traversed my withdrawn isolation. Toward the age of thirteen I conceived a very pure passion for a companion whose beautiful melancholy eyebrows I loved."

"I was scarcely eight," Vally interjected, "when I amused myself maddening little boys with the disquieting and almost expert kisses of my infantile lips. I didn't love them, but I took pride in their precocious disturbance."

San Giovanni turned her eyes toward disappeared days again.

"I composed my first verses for that companion with the lovely eyebrows, who gave me her ignorant tenderness candidly. I resolved to run away with her later when we had both attained the respectable age of liberty. I dreamed of disguising myself as a man in order to marry her. But no carnal image was mingled with that chimera of a narrowly united existence. I only evoked the peace of hours dissolved in one another like harmonious colors.

"For a long time, the ardor of pity burned me. For a long time, like Ione, I feared the unknowable. Today, I take pleasure in the sad grandeur of Uncertainty . . .

"Perhaps I was created for the Apostolate," she said, regretfully, after a pause. "I would have liked to found a religion or rediscover a very ancient and obscurely wise worship—the primitive cult of the Mother Goddess, which once conceived Space and gave birth to Eternity. I don't have the soul of a lover, in spite of the sensual wrath of my poems. I have the soul of a nun, who, having not found peace in the sanctuary, has rejected the veil and weeps on seeing herself naked among the ritual perfumes."

A sadness broke her voice.

"I'm getting lost in a labyrinth of digression," she went on. "Before turning fourteen, then, I was nothing but an idle and nasty animal."

"Like all children," I anticipated.

"Certainly," said San Giovanni, "but my dream infiltrated through the slumber of my being during a journey

I made to Italy. I brought back the confused perception
of beauty. At the age of ten my unconscious soul had
been wonderstruck by the Old Testament and Hellenic
mythology. However, universal splendor had not been
revealed to me, as it was by those landscapes steeped in
luminous perfumes. It was there that I glimpsed amour
more clearly."

"You say that you don't have the soul of a lover, San
Giovanni," I interjected, with a slight astonishment.
"Initiate us into your conception of tenderness and
sensuality."

San Giovanni smiled, with her bizarre demi-smile.

"I've told you how far my childhood was from indecent reveries. At seventeen, I was still totally ignorant of
sexual bestiality, in spite of the Anglo-Saxon liberty of my
reading. A young French friend, whose narrow education
had been very diligently supervised, described the ani-
mality of couplings to me. I listened with an amazed and
initially incredulous disgust. Instinctively, I baulked at the
grotesque ugliness of human rutting. Ulterior reflections
did not dissipate my nausea.

"I soon absorbed myself in less repugnant thoughts,
however. A great thirst for justice enfevered me chimerically. I exalted myself on behalf of the misunderstood
woman subjugated by imbecilic masculine tyranny. I
learned to hate the male, for the base ferocity of his laws
and his impure morality. I considered his work and judged
it bad. For the revolt of the proud individual against oppression was already growling within me.

"It was then that I composed my poem *Vashti*, in
which I celebrated one of the initial feminine rebellions.[1]

---

1 A translation of Renée Vivien's prose-poem "Le Voile de Vashti"

Vashti, the first wife of Ahasuerus, more beautiful and prouder than the timid Esther, once dazzled my juvenile imagination. I admired the magnanimity of her defiance when Ahasuerus ordered her to unveil her face, as glorious as the face of the sun, before the drunken courtiers. She refused to allow her mysteriously splendid visage to be profaned by the lubricious gazes of satraps, and preferred to die, repudiated and wretched.

"And it's for that nobility of soul that I venerate her and love her."

San Giovanni fell silent momentarily. I hastened to interrogate her about the mystery of her amorous life. "Tell us about your tender companion with the beautiful eyebrows, O perverse Saint."

San Giovanni looked away, evasive and fugitive.

"You're mistaken about the ambiguity of that puerile fervor. Ignorance kept our excessively ingenuous mouths apart.

"I was twenty years old before glimpsing the inexpressible grace of feminine amours, that purity in lust, that candid grace in temptation. Reading *Méphistophéla* opened unsuspected gardens to me and the road to unknown stars.[1] I adored that book, in spite of the bad taste of certain chapters in which bourgeois morality espouses popular melodrama in righteous marriage. I understood from then on that uncertain lips could unite without disgust with other lips, more savant but no less timid. I understood that there flourished on earth magical kisses

---

based on the first chapter of the Old Testament book of Esther, can be found in *Lilith's Legacy*, entitled "The Veil of Vashti."

1 *Méphistophéla* (1890) by Catulle Mendès, a lubricious novel about a lesbian *femme fatale*.

devoid of regret and remorse. And with an anxious patience, I awaited the advent of the Unhoped-for . . ."

"Tell us about her, San Giovanni . . ."

But, gripped by the gauche modesty of an ephebe, the poet of Mytilene turned away, and brushed the velvet bass piano with feverish hands. The notes shimmered under the voluptuous hands that stroked them with such light insistence.

"To my inexhaustible regret, I'm not a musician," she sighed. "Music, for me, is only an evocation. And yet, like the Sea, it's Infinity . . . Music is a suggestion. I remember some verses in prose that a morbid nocturne by Chopin dictated to me."

She accompanied herself while speaking, with a tormented melody like the unsteady beat of a feverish pulse.

> *"I love you because you resemble autumn and the sunset. I love you because you are ill. I love you because you are going to die.*
>
> *"I also love you because you have red hair and green eyes, and because you are frail and sad. You have the inflexion of a dying flower. Your voice is as melancholy as the October breezes that lifts up dead leaves.*
>
> *"I love you because you are going to die.*
>
> *"Your lassitude enchants me and your weakness delights me. Someone must surely be waiting for you in the tomb.*
>
> *"For you know, like me, that the Dead, sitting in the depths of their sepulchers, wait for those they have loved. They wait for them stubbornly, without anguish and without impatience, in a frightful immobility.*

"Someone must assuredly be waiting for you in the tomb . . .

"The Dead wrap their fingers around roots, hoping for the coming of their lovers and their companions. And sometimes, through their closed eyelids, they count the years.

"I love you because you are going to die.

"When you are dead, O my Lady of autumn, you will wait for me, sitting on the slabs of leprous marble. You will smile at the patches of mildew that take unexpected forms and strange contours, and which sometimes, like clouds, put on the appearances of terrestrial things. When you are dead, you will wait for me, like the one who is already waiting for me. And beneath your closed eyelids, you will count the years.

"When I sing songs to my shadow, I will sense your thought floating around me, like a cold breath. When the hail rattles against the window, I will hear the drumming of your fingers. The winds of winter will bring me the frisson of your passing shroud. I will know that you are waiting for me, calculating the number of the months and the years.

"Your index finger will cast its shadow on the sundial. You will insinuate yourself through the mist and the drizzle, like the one who is already waiting for me . . .

"I love you because you are going to die.

"It is the brief joy in ephemeral beauty that I drink on your lips. I believe that I am taking

*a little of your fleeting life when I kiss you. I
see through your body the delicate design of the
skeleton. I adore the feverish temples where the
veins are blue and where a dew of cold sweat
shines. I love you, for being so pale . . .*

*"Oh, how beautiful you are, in being so
emaciated and pale!*

*"Someone must surely be waiting for you in
the tomb . . ."*

San Giovanni listened piously to the fugitive echo of
a dying chord.

"The most beautiful thing about that music," she said,
"is the pause in the middle of the rhythm, or the silence
that follows the last tremulous note . . ."

She considered the keys of the mysterious instrument.

"All the charm of the melody is in the play of the left
hand. Oh, that grave sweetness, that inexpressible sadness
of the F key!"

"You have a fervor for sounds, San Giovanni," I observed.

She acquiesced.

"How I love the religious vision that promises future
bliss an Eternal Music! I would like, akin to the Elect, to
be nothing more than a singing breath exhaled in space!"

She resumed, in a voluptuous tone: "Music! What illusion and what magic! I've tried to render that sentiment
in a tale entitled *The Sin of Music*. It's the story of the
temptations of a Saint in the desert. All mirages and all
oases sparkle in vain before his indifferent eyes. Sight does
not doom him. The most marvelous nudities of women
and statues display their splendor before him in vain, like

infernal moonlight on the sand. Even goddesses, more desirable for being distant, allow him to glimpse the white flame of their flesh without causing a covetous gaze to spring from his bleak eyes.

"The perfumes that overwhelm, the perfumes that triumph, the perfumes that kill, rise toward him without interrupting the profound peace of his eremitic body. The fruits most richly impregnated with sunlight, the rare fruits of inaccessible climes, and wines of purple and gold, do not awaken the joy of savor in him. And the most delicate and most disturbing sense, the sense of Touch, is not revealed to him by the animal softness of furs, over which the fingers wander curiously, nor by the fabrics whose equivocal attraction seems a hesitant appeal.

"But he succumbs by virtue of Hearing. Music, as ardent and perfidious as a mistress; Music, which stimulates regrets and reanimates memories; Music, which envelopes and seduces like water, bears his soul away in the sob of a chord. The sensuality of sounds is so acute that it makes him renounce paradisal light.

"Thus the Hermit, once invulnerable, is damned by the Sin of Harmony."

San Giovanni's fingers, expertly belated, caressed the consenting notes with a perverse tenacity.

V
[Beethoven. Op. 14.]

I was twenty years old and intoxicated by young liberties when Ione took me to Vally's house and I knew the ecstatic pangs of the first passion. Since that day of azure and darkness, amity had been effaced by amour. Ione, the pale sister, retreated into the distance. I no longer called her my Consoler, for I no longer confided my sadness to her. I kept it jealously in the painful profundities of my soul. And it was thus that I became a being of silence and solitude.

Vally was entirely given to the changing ecstasy of the moment. Multiple feminine visions succeeded one another in her nuanced existence. I accustomed myself to their odorous presence, to their smiles that asked for my forgiveness. I learned not to harbor any resentment; they did not steal from me a tenderness that I had never possessed. I felt an almost amorous indulgence for my rivals. They tortured me so involuntarily and with such grace!

I recall those passers-by without bitterness. They were adorably dissimilar. Most of all I admired an Israelite as magnificent as the Orient. Her hair was impregnated with an odor of faded roses and sandalwood. Bathsheba unclad could not have been more victoriously splendid. Beneath the languor of her heavy eyelids slumbered the violence of lust. She was almost terrible by virtue of being beautiful.

A child succeeded her, whose profile and avian chirping moved me. She was soon forsaken for a young Englishwoman with the soul of a little girl mounted in the body of a goddess.

Two sisters then disputed Vally's mobile heart. Both were as palely blonde as a boreal sun. But their reign was of short duration. The uncertain lover forgot them, smitten with a young American with a desirable amorous smile. None of them was able to retain her fugitive thought or fix her indecisive heart.

Nevertheless, I envied those puerile beloveds, for they had had from her, if only for an instant, a sincere kiss.

"I don't love you," she said to me in her moments of honesty. "Perhaps I shall learn to love you later. You might gradually teach me forbearance and tenderness."

And, with a dolorous patience, I lay in wait for the tender gaze for which I waited in vain for such a long time.

Summer enfevered the roses, summer radiated over the seas, and Vally intimated to me the order to accompany her to America. I went with her, as on the day when I had abandoned my hopes and my memories for her.

We went to a vast college of women, to which only a few studious men and laborers were admitted. It was an entire sacred city, a city of effort and meditation. Those young women were preparing for the future struggle, where, for their contentment, an infinity of studious dreams was elaborated. The joy of the intellect, a thousand times more poignant than the joy of the flesh, brightened those frank faces inexpressibly. A quietude was exhaled from walls filled with laborious buzzing reminiscent of beehives.

Whoever has not spent the divine month of October in the New World does not know the splendor of autumn. The flame of a universal sunset was before me. The forests burned like bloody pyres, the golds and browns had a dreamlike intensity. Minuscule snakes, greener than molten emeralds, lay dormant amid the dust of the roads, and suddenly became animated like living branches.

In the environs of the city, simultaneously active and contemplative, there was a little cemetery where bats with blue wings came to roam. In that narrow city of the dead, Vally and I caught San Giovanni *in flagrante delicto* in literary composition. She was sitting on the venerable tomb of Hannah Jane, beloved wife of Ebenezer Brown.

"You've realized your ideal of happiness, O poet," mocked Vally, smiling. "Serpents, bats, tombs and solitude: here you are in possession of your paradise. For bliss or damnation differ in accordance with souls."

"Indeed," I approved. "My own heaven is contained entirely within the word Music and my hell in the word Discord. My eternal torture would undoubtedly be to hear aggressive sounds, the grating of saws, the rumbling of trams, the howls of babies, the cries of sirens and the groping of inexperienced pianists.

"I once read a very curious book, *Letters From Hell*,"[1] said San Giovanni, meditatively, "That correspondence of the damned revealed a deplorable Protestant mind, but

---

1 A posthumous fantasy translated from the Danish, *Letters from Hell* (1866), initially signed "M. Rowel" (a pseudonym of the clergyman Valdemar Adolph Thisted) was a best-seller in its day; it is said to have influenced both Hans Christian Andersen and C. S. Lewis.

it abounded in bizarre details about infernal mores and customs. The soul is punished down there by the belated need to expiate terrestrial sins. Egotists wander through the twilight with a dolorous thirst to love and to devote themselves. They stammer futile words of tenderness to the void. They open their arms in vain loving impulses; and the shades on whom they lavish their obsequious offers and fervent caresses push them away in annoyance. Hypocrites are forced to sob their former lies in spite of the protestations of their souls, thirsty for frankness. The torture of the vain is even more terrible. They are condemned to see what others think of them and to hear everything that was said about them during their terrestrial existence."

We shivered in simulated horror.

"What is the punishment of the lustful?" I asked, with interest.

"They are constrained to the act of desire," San Giovanni replied. "Wearied to the point of disgust, they dream obscurely of an impossible chastity. An ardor for solitude gnaws them like hunger and burns them like thirst."

She collected herself momentarily.

"There was once a man who was damned for a woman," she continued. "The sensual ferocity of his amour tortured him even in Eternity. He cherished the hope of rediscovering his wife. Without respite he desired her advent in the Tenebrous Anguish. And for long years he waited."

"Such is the magnanimity of amour," I observed, very philosophically.

"He could still see her, implacably beautiful in all her youth. He panted after the distant lips, bloodied by kisses, the purple eyelids and the inexpressible body. He remembered mysterious evenings, spoken words and divine silences.

"He waited for a long time.

"She finally rejoined him. She crouched at his side. The shadow revealed the face covered by a network of wrinkles. The toothless smile opened over blackened gums. The breasts were like two punctured balloons. The eyes blinked lamentably behind the rare lashes.

"The torture of the lover is to pursue that specter, which he abhors, to sob the confessions of old and to reiterate the promises and the prayers. He implores with repugnance the kisses of that mouth with fetid breath. And he exhausts himself inventing abject praises before that once-desired flesh."

Vally turned away, slightly pale.

"When you descend in your turn into the Eternal Abyss, San Giovanni," I put in, "You'll find many readers there. Your works will be in the hands of all the literate dead."

"You're flattering me. I have a more modest idea of my literary vogue. To be read in hell: what success! That would compensate me for the restricted sale of my volumes down here."

"Justice," I added, "weary of vagabonding vainly on the terrestrial sphere, has taken refuge in hell. For justice is the unique virtue of Demons."

"In hell there are no Demons," said San Giovanni. "Torturers would be futile, since the damned torture themselves. Demons are only the vulgar materialization of Evil Thoughts."

A young professor, whose remarkable Hellenist knowledge Vally esteemed, came to join us in order to announce his engagement to be married, victoriously. Vally murmured a few conventional phrases. San Giovanni considered him, not without melancholy, and said to him amicably:

"I'll offer you, my young colleague, advice that will do more for your future happiness than vain congratulations."

She deployed her manuscript on her knees and chose at random the following passage:

> *The Snake-Charmer said to the ephebe:*
>
> *"This is what the serpents, counselors of sensuality, have taught me:*
>
> *"Flee the act of initiation, as cowardly as pillage, as brutal as rape, as bloody as massacre, and only worthy of a drunken and barbaric soldier.*
>
> *"If the woman you love is a virgin, leave to a stranger the violation of her first modesties. Amour ought to be pure of everything that is not sensuality. Suffering in amour is discordance in music."*

She waited in vain for the emotional thanks of our comrade. With a rare ingratitude, he had gone away as soon as he had heard mention of the act of initiation.

Vally stifled scandalized laughter.

"What advice for a Hellenist fiancé! You've offended the modesty of that worthy young man."

"Too bad," said San Giovanni, implacably. "He didn't hesitate to offend my modesty with that indecent proc lamation of his engagement. Those are improper details, which one ought to avoid giving in public. Everyone has their particular scruple."

"Shut up," said Vally, smiling. "Or rather, read us that essay, which is headed by the enticing title *The Prostitute*."[1]

"I'll grant your request, but not without warning you that the Prostitute appeared to me the other evening under the features of that Monsieur de Vaulxdame with whom you were waltzing so sinuously, and who has come to traffic his insignificant title for significant dollars."

San Giovanni commenced, solemnly:

Look here, upon this picture, and on this.[2]

The female prostitute passes in the night.
Her face has the haggard fixity of waiting. On her cheeks, the redness of make-up resembles the redness of shame. She passes in the night, hunted like wild beasts, stigmatized by universal reprobation, incessantly under threat of infamous captivity. In perpetual danger of death, she has, suspended above her head, not the sword of Damocles but the vulgar knife of the pimp or the temporary lover. She is an exploited, debased creature, an individual crushed by the burden of prejudice and regulation.
Now, that woman has sold herself, and has sometimes even been sold, like the slaves of the

---

1 The noun is given the masculine gender in the tile, implying that the prostitute is male; in the body of the "essay" itself I have distinguished the gender of the different uses of the noun more brutally.
2 This line is rendered in English in the original. It is a quotation from Hamlet Act 3 Scene 4, addressed by Hamlet to Gertrude.

ancient market. And those who move out of her path name her Prostitute.

The male Prostitute wallows in idleness in dwellings as vast as palaces. Servants clad, according to his caprice, in picturesque livery, carry out his orders silently. The fine grace of his horses attracts eyes that delight in beautiful animal forms. Lust, that realization of all terrestrial dreams, radiates immutably over his path. His desires are incarnate in beauty. Praises burst forth around his pride. He passes by, his forehead in the light, more glorified than a scholar and more than an apostle.

Now, that man has sold himself. But Marriage had sanctified the bargain under the vault of the temple. Solemn rejoicing has saluted the venal act. That man is blessed by religion, honored by mores and protected by the law, and I alone name him Prostitute.

That woman has sold herself by virtue of ignorance or necessity, because the laws of salary are pitiless for the woman who works, and the only feminine métier that permits her to live in ease is that of gallantry.

That man has sold himself because, in spite of the possibilities of lucrative labor, he prefers slackness to effort, and opulence to self-respect. Now, a thousand times more morally degraded than the female Prostitute, a thousand times more despicable, the male Prostitute enjoys all the wealth and all the honors of the earth.

And I alone call him by his true name: Prostitute.

"You're right to criticize the male Prostitute," my Priestess approved. "Which won't prevent me from waltzing with him this evening. I'm forsaking the city of study for a very frivolous ball in a country house. Will you go with me, my *cavaliere servante?*"

"No," I refused, mildly. "I've followed you too often with my eyes, sickened to the soul in seeing you undulate in the arms of those puppets. I've envied your partners in the waltz or the cotillion too dolorously and hated them too grimly. I won't go to the ball, Vally."

"So be it," she said, sulkily, with a pretty shrug of the shoulders. "I'll leave you, San Giovanni, since you prefer to my company that of owls and serpents. Meditate as much as you like on the funeral inscriptions that surround you."

And the rustle of her dress awoke, pitilessly, the silence of dead leaves.[1]

---

1 Natalie Barney, as a rich American heiress, was perennially besieged by English and French adventurers eager to trade the supposed prestige of their titles for her dowry. Her father was extremely keen to see her married, and seemingly glad to grant enthusiastic permission to anyone who took the trouble to ask him for her hand. Lord Alfred Douglas is rumored to have been one of several suitors who attempted to persuade her to marry him, before he married Olive Custance. She seems to have contracted the engagement to Freddy Manners-Sutton in order to keep her father's pressure at bay, presumably with no intention of following through, and abandoned the pretence as soon as he was dead. That did not prevent the misandric Tarn from disapproving strongly of her conduct.

VI
[Liedes Ahnung. Schumann.]

THE soil was reanimated under the kisses of winter. It laughed, like a happy giant, rejoiced by snow, wind and magnanimous frosts. The intoxications of the first cold spells filled the atmosphere with vigor and contentment. I was exalted by the frissons in the air, as sharp as a sensuality.

The end of November brought us back to Paris. I did not experience any of the peace of returning that emanates from a familiar house. Only Vally's hearth, where I was, however, the taciturn presence that is tolerated, but which irritates, gave me an impression of wellbeing.

Paris! The name of the beloved and desired city only rendered life to ungracious apparitions: the phantom of the ineffable Petrus, so touching in his fat conceit, and the specters of Vally's innumerable admirers and courtiers, whom I hated *en bloc*.

During my absence, I had not written to Ione. My amorous discouragement was such that I would not have been able to trace a line without tacitly confessing my bitter preoccupations; for Vally's ill-tempered indifference had accentuated over time, and I was beginning to despair. I was so vainly obstinate in an impossible task.

When we returned I went to see the pale friend of my dreamless past. I found her, as always, frightfully meditative. Her immeasurable forehead put a broad white glow in the gloomy room.

For a long time she bathed me with her unforgettably sad and tender eyes. It seemed to me that her eyes expressed the confession of her mysterious thought. I strove at first to decipher her gaze, but my reason lost itself there as in an abyss.

"I beg you," she murmured, in a very soft voice, "understand me. Divine what I can't yet tell you. Divine me and understand me . . ."

My impatient gesture was already responding to her.

"I can't divine you, Ione. I can't understand you. Help me . . ."

She shook her head slowly, with an expression of inexpressible regret. What speech would have been able to translate the mystery of her thought?

"Let's talk about something else. You're not the person of old, so foolishly utopian, so infatuated with ideas and chimeras. You've renounced everything that was once your joy and your pride. Your eyes are two dead lakes and only revive when they encounter Vally's eyes. When she's with you, you only see her face, you only hear her words, and when she's far away, you still contemplate her and listen to her in thought. You're no longer anything but a wandering shadow, you're no longer anything but the reflection and echo of Vally."

I had a long astonished frisson. She had never spoken to me overtly about my disastrous amour.

"You haven't found happiness . . ."

I tried to smile.

"No, certainly not. I have a soul so divinely unhappy that I wouldn't want to be consoled for anything in the world."

Ione uttered a long sigh.

"And yet, I have a prayer to address to you. I'm quite ill, and above all very weary."

"Wearied by thinking too much, Ione," I interjected. "Oh, I beg you, love, act, weep, live desperately, but don't think any longer with that frightful fixity!"

Without listening to me, almost without hearing me, she continued:

"I'm going to rest for a while, in the beneficent Midi. Down there, there are fir trees with pink flowers, and mauve wisterias that fall all the way to the ground. One can contemplate olive groves there the color of waves at twilight, and one can respire inexpressible aromas of orange blossom. In the mountains, the grass is blue with violets. Huge beds of algae turn the sea red. The sun there is so powerful that it dissipates all ills. Come down there to forget. I'll cure you. As before, I'll be your consoler. Come down there . . ."

It seemed to me that all the stars were going out at once in a miserable night. Quit Vally, if only for a few weeks! I almost smiled at the folly of the thought. The excessively suave image looked up in the depths of the evening. I contemplated, in a décor of memory, the cruel blonde hair and the cruel blue eyes that rendered me so feeble and so cowardly . . .

I wanted to refuse the amicable offer affectionately. But I saw such a reckless supplication in Ione's eyes that I dared not formulate the definitive sentence.

"Later," I replied, evasively. "I'll come later, Ione. For the moment, I can't tear myself away from my occupations."

I dared not look at my friend. A silence fell between us so vast that it seemed to extend eternally.

"You promise me to come?" said the pale Ione, finally. "You promise to come later?"

The anguish that I divined in her voice made me shudder suddenly. I lied resolutely.

"I promise you, darling."

"Weigh your words well. There's sometimes an ironic deity that obliges the accomplishment of promises made without the intention of keeping them."

That light phrase fell into the luminous darkness like a prophecy.

I took hold of Ione's cold hands. The unspeakable desolation that was weighing upon her oppressed me in my turn. We remained side by side, and the melancholy torpor enveloping us darkened our uncertain thoughts.

We were as sad as the dusk, and like the dusk, we feared the imminent void of the darkness, I have never known a more poignant hour than that dejected and fraternal hour.

VII
[The Death of Yseult. Wagner.]

IONE left a few days later. I received sunlit flowers from her, and a delicate letter that followed them, as a happiness follows a hope.

I sometimes thought about her with an intense anxiety. Then my devouring passion absorbed my entire soul again.

Increasingly, Vally drew away from me. I only saw her at rare and bitter intervals. She was as infatuated with space and liberty as a seagull, and I followed her flight through the open sky from afar.

One evening, I received a note from San Giovanni. The tormented handwriting extended and launched forth even more feverishly than usual over the pale gray paper.

> *I beg you, use all your influence to put the impetuous Vally on her guard. The Prostitute, very unfortunately, has in his possession a letter from her that contains a formal promise of marriage. I don't believe that Vally has any intention of actually marrying him. American women sometimes amuse themselves by getting engaged* ex improviso, *without attaching any*

The nausea of disgust was even more powerful than my crucified jealousy. I inclined before San Giovanni's hatred of crapulous Man.

Night was falling. I no longer dared go to the house of the excessively insouciant child. The following day, I went to knock on Vally's door. I scarcely looked at the Wood, lacy with frost, like a marvelous Moorish architecture. The imperturbable British footman told me, with all the majesty of the English accent, that his mistress had gone out; but James' solemnity did not succeed in convincing me. I had seen a man's hat and overcoat in the antechamber; and the image of the Prostitute was evoked in my jealous eyes.

"That's all right," I said to James, scandalized to the utmost depths of his footman's soul. "I'll wait for Mademoiselle to return."

And, without paying any heed to social conventions, which I bewildered in the immobile person of the respectable servant, I installed myself in Vally's studio.

The moments passed, heavier than the moments preceding a storm. The door was about to open. Vally would enter in a frisson of perfumes. She would be dressed in moonlight and she would have her necklace of perverse opals around her neck. Her light sleeves would allow a glimpse of the bare arms that I adored.

She would come in and smile at me. What words of voluptuous anger would I find in order to express the hatred of my amour? How would I greet her when she appeared?

The Prostitute was beneath my scorn. He was seeking an establishment; it was his reason for being and his social function. But what about her, my Vally, my amorous virgin and my Priestess?

I wept over her moral decadence more than for herself. What did my miserable everyday torture matter compared with that degradation of the living symbol of my worship?

She was engaged, she had promised everything to that individual with inadmissible sentiments, to that person beneath any insult.

How would I get her when she appeared?

I would not say anything. I would go to her, and I would contemplate the depths of her eyes her cruel blonde soul. She would be frightened by my silence and my calm. Then, coldly and resolutely, I would strangle her . . .

I would strangle her. It would be ugly, brutal and savage, but it would be a brief nightmare, and, in the joy of the mystical murder, I would lie her down on the green divan that resembled a mossy bank. I would dispose around her forehead the halo of her pale hair. I would put the expiatory lilies into her hands, and I would strew over her body the petals of her favorite roses, the white roses with a hint of green. She would sleep, slightly paler than in habitual sleep. And I would love her, in that superhuman moment, more than any human had ever dared to love. It would be Madness, with its exaltations and its terrors, and its afterlife.

I would watch over her until dawn. I would watch the candles vacillate. The azure of midnight would fill the corners with shadow. Vally's eyelids would be strangely blue-tinted. And I would say loudly, like a man speaking in drunkenness: "I have killed her!"

She would remain my virginal Priestess forever. She would be the whiteness of my dreams, the Inaccessible and the Untarnishable.

I would have saved her in saving myself. I would have carried her away in order to contemplate her in Infinity. I would keep throughout eternity her cry of fright—the only sincere cry that I had ever collected from her lying lips—and her vain prayer. She would not know the remorse of having failed herself. She would not know the aftermath of grace, the caricaturish imprints of Time on her human statue. She would be the Beauty that Death eternalizes in a smile. She would not weep for others or for herself. And perhaps she would feel a comprehensive gratitude with regard to the person who had loved her nobly enough to kill her.

The door opened slowly . . . She was about to appear, my dream accomplished . . . And I advanced, my hands clenched in the gesture of strangulation . . . It would be accomplished so quickly, and afterwards . . . afterwards . . .

San Giovanni came in. She did not see my hallucinated eyes, for her eyes were filled with tears.

"I was looking for you," she stammered. "I knew that I would find you at Vally's house. I've just received this telegram . . . Ione . . ."

I tore the banal piece of paper from her hand in which the solemn order of Destiny was intimated: a few words that summarized briefly, stupidly and tragically, the death of two people:

Ione gravely ill. Come.

When I raised my eyes, it seemed to me that I was surging forth, like Alcestis and Lazarus, from funereal depths . . .

"Ione has contracted typhoid fever," San Giovanni continued. "There are redoubtable complications."

"I'm going to Nice," I announced, abruptly. "I only have time for very brief preparations for departure. Make my adieux to Vally."

VIII

[Maestoso andante. Beethoven.]

I went through Ione's garden, where white irises were paling, as sad and pure as lilies. I shall remember those white irises throughout my human existence. A melancholy scent of violets lingered in the pathways, like an adieu.

I considered that garden, where she had doubtless liked to wander, bitterly thoughtful. She had loved those flowers, she had inclined toward those white irises, and she had respired those violets.

It seemed to me that she was already dead. A presentiment stifled the effort of hope within me.

Old words reverberated in the blue silence. San Giovanni had murmured them once on a misty evening.

"Amity is more perilous than amour, because its roots are more profound than the roots of amour.

"The dolor of amity is more bitter than the dolor of amour."

I don't know why those things of the past obsessed me at that moment. The mind sometimes strays in great dolors, it attaches itself to futile things, as someone engulfed by the abyss clutches vainly at a clump of grass.

Something articulated clearly: *You are going to lose Ione. Ione is going to die.*

And I listened without understanding yet.

I picked a white iris. I said: "This flower is going to die, like Ione. It is already dying, like Ione. It is dead, like Ione . . ."

And suddenly, I raised my eyes. A tall black form passed before me. I saw that it was a priest. A great amazement overwhelmed me.

A priest! A priest, among those vehement flowers, in that garden quivering with perfumes. Ione had had a priest summoned to her deathbed. Why?

I remembered certain phrases of mine of which she had approved:

"In my arbors, the flowers are not a symbol. They are only pallors and perfumes. I cannot conceive of any other eternity than that of Poets and Statues . . ."

And that same Ione had had a priest summoned to her!

I evoked my friend's staring eyes, the eyes that seemed no longer able to close, even in slumber, and the forehead *that was still thinking.* I understood all the horror of that perpetual thought. That was what had slowly ravaged and inexorably destroyed Ione's frail body.

I sensed that the poor child, haggard before the impenetrable Mystery, had taken refuge in the human consolation of Catholic belief. The silence had frightened her so abominably that she had listened to the voices that spoke of hope, of certainty, of luminously open skies. Her reason had buckled under the Unknowable, she had attached herself to the faith of the simple individuals who scorn, deny and mock all reason.

And, seeing herself sinking into the darkness, she had sought help in the divine lie that explains the Inexplicable.

That was why the priest had come.

She had once asked me my opinion regarding the afterlife and the soul. I had found nothing to reply to her but the tragic: "*I don't know.*"

And she had sighed profoundly.

"I have no idea," I had said. "I've never had any and I never will have. Ideas pass and change, only sentiments are immortal. Doctrines perish, and amour remains."

I went into the house, which had already taken on the ashen color of funereal dwellings. I insisted on seeing Ione, if only for an instant. And after dolorous supplications, I crossed the threshold of her sickroom.

How can I express the impression that mastered me when I saw her? An immeasurable fear paralyzed within me the dolorous impulse of tenderness.

It was no longer Ione . . . She was already dead. What was agitating and shivering with fever before me was her cadaver, still warm.

Her brown hair, as ardent as autumn nights, had been cut. The poor lips stirred continually for incoherent words. The vague gaze, which no longer discerned anything, turned toward me. Ione contemplated me for a long time—I don't know whether she recognized me. She was no longer anything but an obscure suffering. The frightful enigma of that abolished personality chilled me. And I remained, like Ione, an obscure suffering . . .

For the first time, I understood all the horror of human decadence . . .

Poverty, Malady and Old Age are abysms in which hope is annihilated, because they are irremediable Ugliness.

A terror took possession of me before what had been Ione. Death appeared to me less implacable than that metamorphosis. I no longer had anything but an instinct of flight. That unconsciousness, which could no longer see, which could no longer hear, which could no longer speak, which could no longer understand, like infancy, like idiocy, like extreme old age, was Ione! Ione, that profound subtlety, that thought; Ione, that complex intelligence!

My eyes wandered one last time over that unrecognizable face, over that excessively high and vast forehead that seemed almost deformed to me, so magnified was it on the pale pillow.

I was made to leave, and, like a coward, with my head in my hands, I fled, I fled, I fled . . .

IX
[Funeral March. Chopin.]

THE incoherence of the hours that followed astonishes me and frightens me. I walked for a long time in darkness, groping, like a person suddenly afflicted by amaurosis.

I remember that, in my room, perfumes as sweet as poisons burned my nostrils and throat . . . I could not see anything but Ione's immeasurable forehead . . . The blinking of my eyelids enfevered my sick eyes . . . I became heavily, stupidly drowsy, like a drunken man lying on stones.

. . . And I woke up . . . The room was blue with darkness. A rigid stupor immobilized my haggard thoughts.

Ione, standing at the foot of my bed, was contemplating her hands, in the strange attitude familiar to her. Without looking at me, she retreated to a corner where she was no longer anything but whiteness of mist and dream.

With a painful effort, I tried to get up and go toward her . . . My foot slipped and I fell into a flow of hot lava that was streaming and seething at the foot of my bed. I wanted to cry out in distress, but the fuming river carried me away, a wisp of straw adrift its fiery waves. To either side of the blazing torrent, old women were crouching, cooking rice and eggs over the liquid flame. And the moon was coppery, like a winter sun. Ashes were falling in a dense hail.

An abominable thirst desiccated my palate and throat.

. . . My eyes opened in a temple to the breath of a furnace. A ruby throne reddened the darkness like a setting star. From the height of the throne, Kali contemplated me with a religious ferocity. She dropped the skull that she was crushing in the manner of a hungry bitch and smiled at me with her red teeth . . .

The sirocco carried me away, a whirlwind of burning and yellow dust. The sand and the dust filled my bruised lungs atrociously. I opened my mouth and a strangled gasp shook my breast . . . The sand and the dust were choking me, blinding me and burying me . . .

I cried out in the starless night . . .

Priestesses with fingers steeped in nard were swaying in mystical dances. They were semi-veiled by nocturnal blue fabrics. A vast emerald emphasized each navel, and their uncovered pubis burned with blonde or russet flames. I was a peacock feather that one of them was agitating at the whim of the lascivious dance. That ritual movement shook me implacably . . .

Through the open window of the cottage the voices of passers-by entered. All the infinity of the unknown came in through the window with those voices. But I did not listen to them, my eyes fixed on a white rose that was swaying at the height of the casement.

Then there was a childishly artificial landscape, which evoked the English illustrations of Norwegian and German fairy tales. Varnished trees with painted foliage were aligned to either side of a path smoother than a little girl's hair . . .

And I found myself before Vally's corpse. Vally was floating on a stagnant marsh. Her pale breasts were two nenuphars. The revulsed eyes were *looking at me* . . . I understood that I had drowned her previously, in the stagnant marsh. She was floating, her hair mingled with irises and reeds, like a perverse Ophelia. I had killed her previously, for an insensate motive. And with her eyes, devoid of a gaze, she contemplated me eternally . . .

I felt the cold air of a mortuary crypt on my face. I was standing in the middle of four coffins. The largest was a man's coffin. There was something massive and imposing about it. I understood that it was the coffin of an important man, a politician or a diplomat . . . Flowers devoid of poetry were displayed there in large dark patches: immortelles and heavy pansies with red velvet petals.

Beside that mass, attenuated and diminutive, was an embryonic coffin, the coffin of a larva, bathing in the twilight of limbo. Colorless wreaths, with a very faint scent, were fading there with simplicity. That child's coffin was tragic and null, like everything that might have been.

Frightful funerary stained glass covered a shrunken coffin, the wood of which was furrowed by numerous wrinkles, like cobwebs. Those hideous wreaths of black and yellow pearls were to perpetuate the bourgeois memory of an old woman with a surly voice.

And in the deepest shadow, in perpetual adoration of fervent candles, there was a virginal coffin perfumed by white violets. I understood that I was seeing Ione's coffin.

The silence was so mysterious that even my heartbeats had fallen silent.

But, more frightful than the clarion of divine judgment, the wood of the large coffin was creaking. That was the fermentation of putrescence.

A gasp, and another gasp, and a final gasp . . . I had ceased to exist. I was a soul stripped of its body. I was a formless and confused mass, devoid of limits and consistency. I was floating, having no other sensation than a shiver of nudity.

A thought surfaced in the milieu of that self-conscious void, a thought sharper than desire and prayer: "A personality! A body! A name! Oh, to become someone! To be what I was, although I have already forgotten who I was!"

Darkness . . . and nothingness . . .

X

[Funeral March. Chopin.]

FINALLY, dawn rose in my darkness, and the gray apparition of beings and things replaced the fears of delirium. As soon as I was able to hear human speech, I was told that Ione was dead.

She was reposing in a funeral crypt. Her narrow coffin was adorned with white violets. Through the penumbra, I distinguished, with a great shiver, *three other coffins* like those I had seen in my delirium.

I remained among the dead all day, and only withdrew toward nightfall. The perfume of dying flowers mingled with I know not what insipid odor, which frightened me. At intervals, the wood of the coffins creaked in the silence; a rose shed its petals, with a very soft sound.

When I went back up into the light, everything that I saw seemed incomprehensible and new to me. I resembled the dead more than the living. Voices surprised me with their strange sonorities, the rumble of the carriages in the streets astonished me, and the sight of people struck me with stupor.

One day, someone came to tell me that the funeral would take place the following day.

In a mist of tears, I remember the cold church, and the compassionate crowd, and a few profound dolors. I

can still see the white catafalque and the virginal flowers. I can also evoke the cold British clergyman and the
cold Anglican service. In spite of Ione's conversion to the
Catholic religion, her parents had imposed their will in
the choice of Protestant ceremonies.

The cry of *resurrection* and *eternity* sounded hollow before the coffin, where the pale flowers were fading. I heard,
like a knell dominating the sobs, the liturgical phrase:

Though worms shall eat this body . . .

And the horrible vision of that soft and delicate body
prey to the worms of the sepulcher surged forth to my
misted eyes . . .

Though worms shall eat this body . . .

Those words resounded within me more profoundly
than all the promises of immortality. My pagan soul lamented over the disappeared beauty, the vanished sweetness. I had regret without hope, and Christian consolation
thus appeared to me to be the cruelest mockery.

I fell to my knees. Before whom, before what, and why?
I don't know. I simply knelt down, before something that
was above my dolor, and which I did not understand . . .

God! The poor word, the miserable word that names
the Unnamable! How can a name—which is to say, a label invented by humans in order to recognize themselves
among their fellows, a definition of a human thought—
summarize Infinity?

And what did God and Infinity, and even Eternity,
matter, by comparison with that cadaver, which was a
beloved person?

XI

[The Death of Ase. *Andante doloroso*. Grieg.]

SAN GIOVANNI was right when she said: "The dolor of amity is more bitter than the dolor of amour . . ."

Vally's cruelties never made me suffer as much as the loss of Ione. Her lies had never made me suffer as much as the silence of that dear person, whose last words I had not heard.

What had happened in the depths of that taciturn soul during the last months of her human existence, *I would never know*. I would be eternally ignorant of her dolors; her doubts, her hesitations and her final conversion would be impenetrable for me. She had taken her secret into the darkness. My affection had become foreign to her. I was the frivolous, importunate Past, whom she had not judged worthy of her memory.

But that bitterness was soon forgotten in the face of the beauty of that death. Ione had departed consoled, if only by an illusion, if only by a chimera. She had had the Faith that surpasses Reason.

"She died happy," I sobbed, recklessly. "What does the rest matter? *She died happy*."

Ione, my Consoler, I no longer have any words before the Infinity of your sepulcher, before the dawn of your death. If I could, I would not recall you to mortal existence. I would not extract you from the blissful peace of your slumber. If I dared to envy you, I would envy your repose. But whatever might happen, I will keep your memory, your pure and fresh memory . . .

Ione. O best tenderness of my soul, I have bid you the supreme adieu. Sleep in all serenity, sleep among the chaste souls who resemble you, the souls that no memory of amour will torment in their repose. Sleep in peace, you who were consoling amity, you who were the virginal Tenderness before amour and above amour . . .

Requiescat in pace . . . Amen . . .

XII
[Op. 22. Beethoven.]

*T*HE *evening is as glorious as a hosanna . . .*
      Once it understood me and calmed me.

I weep in contemplating the sky as red as ocher
Over my drifting mind and my mediocre heart.

The feverish memory of a Friend is in the air . . .
The Rainbow of Death is rising over the sea.

And toward you, the Priestess, and me, the disciple.
The Night rises, unique and diverse and multiple.

The color of my days, like an incomplete spectrum,
Darkens gravely from green to violet.

Without revolt, I await the neutral dusk,
Gray sand where footfalls are soft and muffled.

Redder than the wine at the Wedding in Cana,
Here comes the evening that would calm me

Once, and which poured its sulfur and ocher gold
Over my drifting mind and my mediocre heart.

Vally's exquisitely artificial voice modulated those sad verses, which San Giovanni had once dedicated to her.

I went in. My mourning dress put a somber note among the young colors.

My Loreley's attentive audience was contemplating her in all fervor and acclaiming her frenetically. The Prostitute made himself especially noticeable by the excess of his admiration.

Vally, a perverse Madonna of profane chapels, respired the incense of her faithful with a distant mildness.

I have a hatred and horror of writers and all those who participate, directly or indirectly, in the debauchery of print, dishonoring our epoch. So Vally's literary friends hastened to take their leave of her as soon as they saw me come in. Evidently, I put them to flight.

Only the Prostitute confronted the enemy, represented by my humble person. He listened with fervor to Vally's light speech.

"I remember," she said, "a little cousin whom I liked to pound to a jelly. Through his tears he rejoiced in being beaten. The poor child was timid and gentle; he dressed dolls in bright fabrics, which I then decapitated mercilessly."

"How I regret, Mademoiselle, not having known you in that epoch," the Prostitute sighed, imbecilically. "You must have been such an adorable child!"

"He's as banal as adultery," I observed, when the young man finally quit my Loreley's drawing room.

Vally turned her icy eyes toward me. She did not reply directly to that attack.

I continued:

"San Giovanni told me yesterday: 'If I had been unfortunate or imbecilic enough to marry, the reading of the three thousandth novel of adultery would have determined in me the irresistible vocation of faithful wife. Oh, the novel has culpable idylls for the usage of women of the world and little housewives in a bad way!'"

At that moment, San Giovanni's serpentine dress slid over the carpet with a quiver of scales.

"You've arrived a minute too soon or too late," I observed. "The enthusiastic audience that was listening to your verses has just fled, and I was preparing to praise you with a respectful admiration when you arrived. Your presence has dried up the flow of my praise. I won't say any more. I'm listening."

"I've just spent a mystical hour in a very old church," said San Giovanni. "I lingered amid the gray darkness of the nave, and the incense made my brain divinely heavy. In the presence of those silent men and meditative women, the very profound words of a blind man, heard in Tunis, returned to my memory: '*Give me a little money, in order to buy light.*'

"We all forget that light is not for sale. We are the Blind," San Giovanni added, in a muffled voice, "and we exhaust our will pointlessly in the effort to see, instead of closing our eyes and looking into ourselves. The light is within us, not without. We will not see, and ought to resign ourselves to not seeing."

"Oh, to contemplate that which dazzles the fixed pupils of the blind! To hear the sobbing harmonies to which the dead listen in ecstasy!" I interjected. "And above all to dream the incomprehensible and immeasurable dream of the Mad! Dolor has no empire over them. They live in the splendor of an illusory royalty. Others think of being God, and are in truth what they think they are. They are enigmatic and superhuman."

"You talk too much," Vally reproached. "Can't you listen to San Giovanni instead of inflicting on us your futile dissertations on the mad, whom you resemble."

"Don't think you can tell me, Vally . . ."

The door-curtain rose. In a sound of stirred leaves, a Woman appeared to me. My eyes were attracted by the tresses of Melisande, the unreal and red hair of a martyr. She had the distant gaze of the daughters of the North. On seeing her I experienced the divine and terrible frisson that a statue awakens, springing from the radiant marble, a nostalgic painting, or an infinite chord. With a disturbance of my entire soul, I heard a name: Eva.

It was only a vision. The young woman left us almost immediately. The religious charm of her grave voice persisted within me.

We fell silent after her departure. The shadow seemed more mysterious. The effluvium of that inexpressible individual impregnated the atmosphere. There was a solemn mildness in and around Eva.

Vally and the poet resumed chatting, but in lower voices. I soon went out into the tumultuous street. My soul was oppressed by Discord and Noise. The ugliness of the city saddened me. I breathed in with all my strength a freshly green silence, amid lively water and forests.

Suddenly, floating above the confusion, bells spilled out their seraphic notes. They were praising, in unison, a Saint, a Martyr, glorifying the sacred name: Eva! Eva! Eva!

XIII
[Op. 7. Minor. Beethoven.]

"CAN'T you smell a tenacious odor of printer's ink?" asked San Giovanni, her nostrils dilated.

The ocellated sunset entered through the windows of her study.

"Undoubtedly," I acquiesced. "Isn't that the most subtle incense that can flatter a literary Divinity . . . ?"

"Shut up," said San Giovanni. "I'm nauseated by everything expressed in verse or prose."

"Me too," smiled my Priestess.

Disdainfully, she turned to me.

"Do you know why I take pleasure in the company of the amiable gentleman that you call, ridiculously, the Prostitute? Because he pronounced to me the other day the exquisite remark: '*Mademoiselle, I never read.*' If I had the possibility of loving within me, I would have devoted a profound passion to him for that remark, sprung from blissful ignorance as from a clear spring."

"Why do you write, San Giovanni?" I asked, astonished. "That weakness afflicts me in an individual as intelligent as you. It's a pastime like any other, superior to the art of massacring flies, but an amusement devoid of grace, as you recognize yourself."

"I don't know what occult power makes me obstinate in the vain work of wearying my readers and disgusting myself," she sighed. "I'm the prey of a nasty habit, like a drunkard or a morphine addict. What philanthropist will found a sanitarium where incurable litterateurs could be cured of their hideous malady, by means of hygiene, remedies and intelligent care?

"You think I'm joking," she added. "I never joke. Joking is a vulgar masculine invention. I tell you in all sincerity: I have a disgust for the métier of writer."

She smiled.

"Only yesterday, did not an imbecile offend my most sacred modesties by addressing a letter to me whose subscription made me shudder with a just indignation: *Mademoiselle Willoughby, Woman of letters?*

"That is cynical. One doesn't advertise such turpitudes. Would one put in the post an envelope formulated thus: *Mademoiselle Maximilienne de Château-Fleuri, Prostitute?*

"As the enlightened public has, for both professions, which are both very interesting and necessary, the same indulgent scorn, I demand at least in favor of women of letters the same elementary politeness that one accords to renowned demi-mondaines."

"It's because the woman of letters has infinitely less modesty than the courtesan," I hazarded. "One only sells her body to what is, in sum, a restricted number of individuals; the other sells her soul, in a print run of thousands. The naked soul is more indecent than the unclad body."

"You're as stupid as the people who write to me. I can't imagine a worse insult to throw in someone's face. Anyone can write about my work anything they like, but to address agreeable buffoonery of this sort to me . . ."

She unfolded a letter, laughing.

Mademoiselle,
I regret not finding in your work the trace
of a masculine influence. Is not getting closer to
nature the greatest ambition that a writer can
conceive?

"The best way of getting closer to nature, in writing," Vally put in, "is to make spelling errors."

I looked at San Giovanni compassionately. "I admit that that missive is in the worst bad taste. It can only come from a university professor or a librarian."

"One ought not to celebrate in literature that which is inauthentic," said Vally, corroboratively, "and a man is Inauthenticity *par excellence*. If there is only a small number of female writers and poets, it is because women are too often condemned by convention to celebrate man. That is sufficient to paralyze in them any effort toward Beauty. Thus, the only female poet, whose immortality is similar to the immortality of statues, is Psappha, who did not deign to perceive masculine existence. Her work bears neither the trace not the pollution of it. For she celebrated *the sweet language and desirable smile* of Atthis, not the muscular torso of the imaginary Phaon."

San Giovanni contemplated my perverse beloved with the gratitude we experience for those who express, certainly less well than ourselves but in another way, our most sacred theories.

"I'm not at the end of my troubles," she continued. "Read this article by the secretary of *Action Provinciale*, which I've just received. The banality of its style is spiced by a savantly whimsical orthography. It's regrettable that the fact of writing *filzofy* instead of *philosophy* cannot cast an illusion over poverty of expression and wretchedness of thought. This Monsieur Bellebotte de Foyn, like all petty provincials of letters, is puffed up by an immense vanity. As much as Petrus he esteems, smiling at himself in the mirror, that the seduction of the male is so irresistible that no woman could remain insensible to so much charm. Let me read you this ineffable sentence:

"'Sappho, truly human, ultimately burns for the *veritable* amour, the amour *natural* for humans, the *inevitable amour*, instead of morbid and abnormal lust . . .'"

"The language of a provincial romantic boor," said Vally, smiling and shrugging her shoulders.

"That monsieur is very sympathetic to me," I intervened. "The distinction of his stupidity pleases me as much as the naïve quavering of his outmoded style."

"One only burns for amour any longer in the verses of Abbé Delille," acquiesced the perverse Madonna of profane chapels.

"The morning post," San Giovanni confided to us, "brought me this missive from an individual who, after gratifying me with the most excessive and absurd praise, asks for my photograph! Read it."

She handed me a letter bearing the postmark of a provincial city. I read:

> *Madame and dear enchantress,*
>
> *Can even a Goddess be offended by being adored, above all when, like you, one sees her celebrating the caress? Since I have studied your works, I carry with me your gracious vision,*

*but every dream needs an aliment of reality. I
do not ask to descend with you into the Elysian
depths in order to love there for an hour; what I
implore from you is to send your portrait . . .*

"Have you given a lesson in politeness to that inhabit-
ant of a little city where there is a dearth of women?" Vally
asked.

"Would you like to read my response? I haven't yet put
it in the post."

Monsieur,

*Know that it is always very dangerous to
write to people whose character and existence
one does not know, and that you have, indeed,
chosen your correspondent badly. I do not send
my portrait to strangers. Far from taking pride
in masculine homages, I consider them as an
offense and an insult.*

*You ought to have understood, not being
ignorant of my theories of grim independence,
that I would never have had the simplicity of
marrying. The title of Madame that you inflict
upon me disobliges me infinitely.*

*You tell me, Monsieur, that you "do not ask
to descend with me into Elysian depths." You
only lacked that! Because one has the misfor-
tune to write in verse and prose, even when one
is "celebrating the caress," according to your
elegant expression, it does not necessarily follow
that one must be a facile woman.*

*Accept, Monsieur, my sentiments of pro-
found surprise.*

"I understand your indignation," I approved, "but do you have other subjects of bitterness, O Muse who lives celebrating the caress?"

"Certainly. The director of a provincial rag has sent me a postcard in which he informs me that, having inserted in his revuette a favorable critique of my work, he has seen several of the *Aquitaine Littéraire*'s subscribers cancel their subscriptions."

"Perhaps that monsieur does not know that you have enjoyed thus far the esteem of your concierge. He does not suspect that his open letter might have the most unfortunate effect on the mind of that dignitary."

San Giovanni went on, wrathfully:

"Here is another passage from another letter in the same genre. It's the response of a critic whom I had informed that he was mistaken in gratifying me with the title of Madame."

> *How could I suppose that the title of Madame would offend you? Your disgust for men I attributed to experience, of course. By what right, in fact, can one condemn in a pitiless manner a sex of which one is ignorant?*

"What a plebeian style!" I objected.

"He's a maladroit myopic," observed my Very Blonde. "One can, without being the wife or lover of a man, judge the entire sex by its actions and its words. Now, the actions of men always have the unique objective of subjugating a woman to their stupid caprice, their sensuality and their unjust and ferocious tyranny. How can one not hate an individual who presents himself to you in the species of a master? Any intelligent and proud individual necessarily revolts against the yoke of another, sometimes her equal but more often than not her inferior?"

"That hirsute face, reminiscent of a gorilla, would suffice to distance me from masculine amour," San Giovanni interjected. "I once dreamed that I was afflicted by a beard. I shall never forget the fear and disgust with which I contemplated myself in a black mirror, a mirror of darkness."

She stopped, and then, very convinced: "Oh, the ugliness of men!"

"But among all these rather discouraging missives," I insisted, "there must, however, be expressions of admiration to be found."

In San Giovanni's distant eyes two red gleams burned.

"Don't talk to me about those false admirations, which are only a shameful mixture of unhealthy curiosity and agreeably tickled vice!" the poet protested. "I prefer all the attacks, even the insults, to those admirations. My self-esteem repudiates them and my pride is offended by them. The impudence of those praises is only equaled by their inanity. Men only see in the love for a woman a spice with which to relieve the insipidity of habitual rites. As soon as they take account of the fact that that worship of grace and delicacy does not admit any equivocation or sharing, they rebel against the purity of the passion that excludes them and scorns them.

"For myself," she added, almost solemn by virtue of sincerity, "I have exalted the amour of noble harmonies and feminine beauty to the extent of a Faith. Any belief that inspires ardor and sacrifice is a veritable religion."

196

"All religions are veritable, and yet none is true," I regretted.

"Except mine," affirmed San Giovanni.

She continued, her expression darkening:

"I don't know why the dolorous métier of woman of letters weighs upon me more heavily than usual today. Prostitutes who, in spite of the ugliness of their existence, have not forgotten all impulse toward the Better, must suffer similar nauseas. Their repugnance is no more repellent than mine. You're right, my obscure conscience, I've sold my soul. But the punishment for my ignorance is in these so-called admirations that address the woman more than the artist. I no longer aspire to the honor of being stoned. Oh, to encounter a fraternal comprehension, without astonishment and without praise: a mute feminine comprehension that would console me for all the words read and heard!"

"How I approve of you," sighed Vally. And, looking in my direction: "You will never be for me the incarnation of that unsuspectably sweet sympathy, because you love me without understanding me and you admire me blindly. With all my weary soul. I aspire to that unknown amity. With all my glutted soul, I turn toward it in the hours of twilight."

"If I have confounded your image, my Priestess, with the image of the Divinity that you serve, and whose mysterious religion you have taught me, it is because I can neither love nor hate by halves. I love you with an absolute amour. I love your injustices and your treasons as much as your magnificent impulses. I don't deny that my passion is blind. It abandons itself without discernment. But while I offer you the best and worst of myself, you demand an impossible amity of me."

Vally was not listening to me.

"As for you, San Giovanni," she said, "you have all my sympathy. I don't admit that the personality of the artist should be mingled with the work that she elaborates in suffering. The public espionage organized around the life of a writer, I condemn as the equal of the cowardly profanations of sepulchers that biographies and posthumous publications are."

I addressed Vally:

"More than any other rebellious and sincere mind, I sense the immensity of that cry of amour: *Get thee to a nunnery.* No one has known like Hamlet the vomit of people and things. Quivering with regal wrath, he wanted to preserve from exterior pollution the woman he loved, and to cloister her in the dignity of solitude."

"*Be thou as chaste as ice, as pure as snow, thou shalt not escape calumny,*"[1] underlined the poet of Mytilene. "I've often dreamed of the coolness of chapels, as one dreams of Death. I've suffered all my life from a lack of faith; for the only enviable happiness is that of nuns, hermits and solitaries."

"I share your opinion," confirmed my Loreley. "The amorous are predestined to multiple anguish; for men are involuntarily scornful of those who bend to their yoke. Like sly animals they like to be beaten. That is the most profound instinct that speaks within them. Thus they only ever adore the woman who disdains them. In fact, San Giovanni, has any woman ever loved a man?"

"I have difficulty conceiving such a deviation of feeling. Sadism and the rape of small children appear infinitely

---

1 Given in English in the original; Hamlet addressing Ophelia in *Hamlet* Act 3, Scene 1.

more normal to me. The likes of Juliet, Yseult and Héloïse loved amour, they didn't love the lover."

"Permit me, O equivocal Saint . . ." I began.

Vally darted a suspicious glance at me. "You have the ridiculously solemn expression of someone about to give advice," she stung.

"I'll respond to you with a quotation, my Very Blonde. Do you remember the Charmer of Serpents, whose maxims our literary friend transmitted to us?

"*Never follow advice, even one of those that I give you. Every individual ought to live their personal life and pay dearly for the experience that proves nothing.*"

"So be it," Vally conceded, "but that won't prevent you from inflicting on us the advice to which we won't listen."

"No longer receive any litterateur, San Giovanni. Close your door to authors as to critics. Only then will you enjoy the peace of the wicked. For the just don't savor peace; their conscience torments them."

"You're disagreeable and hateful, like all those who reason."

XIV

[Adagio sostenuto. Beethoven.]

I was wandering the streets crimsoned by a marvelous mauve dusk when I encountered San Giovanni. She seemed more than ever to have been detached from an ancient frame. The breasts and hips devoid of relief, of an adolescent virgin or ephebe, did not lift up the fabric of her imprecise dress. She was as straight and tall as a page.

"What benevolent hazard has led your steps here, San Giovanni? What Florentine with eyes darker than the Italian night, tuning a lute or shredding a rose, are you doubtless waiting for?"

The Androgyne replied to me brusquely, entirely given to the disturbance of her soul.

"I believe that at the bottom of your bitter passion for Vally, a tenderness that you do not suspect yourself lies dormant. I've come to appeal to the mildness of amity that is within you."

My strange friend paused, indecisively.

"You don't know Vally as I do. Your British soul, in which the old Protestant leaven is still slumbering, can't yield to the intelligence of these very bold and very ingenuous flirtations in which the childishly perverse debauchery of American women take pleasure. Your races have different souls; you will never understand one another. Vally likes to make men suffer by impudently offering them her inviolable beauty. She has cultivated the attitude of a tangible and yet distant Idol. She quivers delightfully in knowing herself to be inaccessible in an atmosphere of desire and covetousness. She adores the tortures to which her gaze and her smile give birth. The sentiment of her feminine power intoxicates her; but she remains colder than the eternal ice that defies the sun. Your Saxon pride will never admit those subtleties. You retain the hostile soul, bristling with suspicions, of the ancient Roundhead."

She paused, her enigmatic eyes scrutinizing my humiliated eyes.

"Listen to me carefully, disciple of the Ironside Cromwell, so little understood by the Frenchman Hugo. If you do not moderate your jealous dolor and your grim humor, *you will lose Vally*. She will escape from the fog with which you want to envelop her and in which she's stifling. She needs the open air, space and sunlight. She has such a burning youth, such an ardor for life!"

"Oh, San Giovanni, patron of perverse amours, advise me, for no one knows Vally more fraternally than you."

"Vally, as you know, has made the mistake of becoming secretly engaged to the Prostitute. Oh, don't attribute more importance to that insignificant fact than it has in reality. The majority of young American women, I've already told you a hundred times, promise marriage right and left without the slightest intention of accomplishing that sacrifice. It's a pretext for kisses on the lips, nothing more, and in America, a kiss on the lips has scarcely more gravity than a kiss on the cheek in France. Between sisters and between friends, without equivocation, they kiss one another on the mouth. Vally is only following the customs of her native land. She has already had thirteen fiancés, and it's doubtless in order not to stop on that fatal figure that she's chosen a fourteenth . . ."

San Giovanni hesitated momentarily.

"I beg you, obtain from our eccentric Morgana the promise to banish that man from her intimacy. I won't pronounce the outmoded and ridiculous word 'compromise.' Young women are no longer compromised, thank God. They alone can compromise themselves by going to live maritally with a man or becoming pregnant. Vally will never give herself to a man," she continued. "She doesn't like men, you ought to know that as well as I do. She mistrusts them, as one instinctively mistrusts one's adversaries; she hates them like enemies, and measures herself against them as with rivals. Have no fear of the presence of a man in Vally's heart."

I was no longer listening to San Giovanni's words; I could no longer see the smile on the sinuous lines of her lips. I tottered, intoxicated by dolor.

"Addio, perverse Saint."

Without thinking, I went toward Vally's house. I was astonished to be suffering so little, or, rather, to be suffering unconsciously.

On arriving at the door at which I had hesitated delectably so many times before entering, the horror of the present recalled me to the reality of the moment, as a new torture reanimates a fainted patient.

I no longer remember very precisely what followed, for I was walking in a mist of nightmares. Above all, my memory evoked the savant penumbra of the green boudoir and the white silhouette of Vally.

On seeing me, the crease of her lips designed a constrained smile. The Prostitute was agitating feverishly in his armchair.

I approached Vally.

"I've come to congratulate you on the happy event of which I've just learned. Your engagement . . ."

Vally stood up, as white and tall as an expiatory lily.

"I don't understand," she said, dryly. "There has never been any question of engagement between Monsieur de Vaulxdame and me."

When I recovered the notion of real things, the Prostitute was no longer in the boudoir. Vally was looking at me with her coldly wrathful blue eyes.

I don't know what awkward words I stammered in my fever. I attempted, mechanically, phrases of reproach and criticism, striving to maintain a resolute tone. My Loreley's thin lips contracted. They seemed no more than a thin horizontal line in her motionless face. I listened to myself without hearing myself.

Vally's voice, as hard as a metallic impact, striped the silence.

"I can't explain your imbecile obstinacy in irritating me and rendering yourself intolerable. You must have seen that, although I disdain calumnies, I scorn those who make themselves the stupid echo on them. I don't believe a word of these ridiculous fables regarding Monsieur de Vaulxdame, doubtless invented by your delirious jealousy. But this perpetual enervation into which you take pleasure in throwing me with your cantankerous and absurd suspicions has wearied my patience. We're at a turning of Destiny where our different routes separate. I've always been honest with you. I haven't made you deceitful protestations of tenderness. From the first moment, I opened the emptiness of my heart to you. I would have liked to love you; you haven't been able to inspire in me the amour for which I've wished so vainly."

"I don't know whether my maladroit passion has been the sole cause of the great misunderstanding of our souls. Certainly, I've importuned you with my umbrageous suspicion. But was it not the logical consequence of the scornful coldness that you testified to me? You address yourself to me like a brutal master bullying a negligent servant. You take pleasure in wounding me and giving your courtiers the spectacle of my humiliation. Although those multiple wounds were more precious to me than the caresses of another, they were as bitter to me as the end of terrestrial hopes.

"I'm not making you any reproach, Vally, my Very Blonde and my Beloved. I have immolated my life to you joyfully. You have enabled me to know the incomparable sensuality of sacrifice, the marvelous sweetness of renunciation. I have loved you with a pious amour, as others love their Madonna. In truth, the priests and nuns who repudiate the century in their divine fervor have not known the mystical ecstasy with which I have abandoned everything to follow you. You are the Unforgettable, Vally. You can expel me from your presence, you can exile me from your cruel grace, but you can never efface the incomparable memory that I have put in shelter of the metamorphoses of existence, for you can never efface the profound burn of the first amour."

She was no longer listening to me. A glacial anger shone in her eyes, as palely blue as a Northern river.

"Your presence has become odious to me," she said, in the measured voice of judges pronouncing a capital sentence. "You are, on my road, the shadow that obscures the radiance and puts the roses in mourning. Your acrid sadness exasperates me unspeakably. The bitterness of your character renders you abominable. You are a soul of anger and hatred. You are obstinate in seeing me in the least beautiful aspect. Everything that I possess of pride and nobility has remained unknown to you. Your paltry jealousy cannot rise above events and appearances. Go, I prefer no matter what honest intimacy to the hypocrisy of your amour. Go!" she ordered, in her voice of steel.

I went. A great silence fell within me. My heart was like a sepulcher without a dawn.

XV
[Op. 2, no. 2. *Largo appassionato, lento sempre.*
Beethoven.]

I left the next day for Toledo. I love the attitude of that autumnal city, lingering in memory. I love the leprosy of its houses, the malady of its pavements, the wounds of its walls, and the agony of its frescoes. The love of madness drew me toward El Greco's paintings. His angels of dementia, with bizarre receding brows, from which thought has fled forever, obsess me with their hallucinatory gazes. In Madrid I had contemplated for hours the long implausibly narrow and pale faces of his portraits.

Whence comes to me that singular passion for madness and suicide, when I possess neither enough imagination for the one, nor enough courage for the other? I don't know . . .

So, I did not have the definitive bravery for the one Act that is worth a resolution. The complexity and ugliness of means of deliverance retained me, and above all the dread of the ridicule that stigmatizes abortive suicides.

The memory returned to me of a morbid litany that San Giovanni had once composed in honor of Our Lady of Fevers, so victoriously mounted in a reliquary in that city of desolation.

Your fetid breath has corrupted the city . . .
A green of gangrene, a green of poison
Swarms, and night crawls like a reptile.
The crowd recites a prayer in chorus,
A fervent delirium burning the lips,
A glacial frisson amid the sweat,
Toward your lividity, Our Lady of Fevers!

Shadow has consecrated its evil gleam to you,
The blue phosphors are your frail candles,
And the fire follets gild your altar,
Virgin who smiles at the death of virgins,
Who remains deaf to the obscure appeal,
Madonna to whom matins and vespers
Rise up shivering, Our Lady of Leprosies!

Your cathedral, with walls corroded by lichens
Sickens the evening with its vapid warmth.
On the soiled beds of hideous couplings,
The moisture of sick hands sweats
Scaly lepers and the moribund
Mingle their sighs with the shrieks of ospreys
And kiss your knees, Our Lady of Wounds!

Your tragic elect have inclined their foreheads
Beneath the divine wind of your litanies,
And amid the incense and the sacred songs
And the flow of acrid fluids,
Exhale a reek of pestilence.
The pus and the blood and pale tears
Have blessed your naked feet, Our Lady of Gasps!

Gradually, I discerned the cruel pallor of the Madonna of plagues. In her stagnant eyes, the reflections of dead waters were tinted with blue and green. Paludal breaths emanated from the tormented pleats of her robe. Her face was as tumultuous as the visions of delirium. But what frightened me the most is that I recognized in the Mortal Image the image of Vally. The stagnant eyes reflected Vally's eyes. The changing face was similar to Vally's face. She had come to corrupt the air and the sunlight in which I was steeping my sobbing lassitudes. She had come to poison forever my hopes of forgetfulness and cure. She had come, knowing that I would not escape her . . .

The days went by, and I wrote to San Giovanni in order to abridge a dolorous hour.

> *She haunts me like a remorse. I can no longer get a grip on myself, I can no longer revive. Her memory is killing me without finishing me off.*
>
> *I hear mention of her. She is joyful. She is amusing herself, back there. She has no thought outside her futile balls and dinners, and it is of no importance to her that I'm agonizing here.*
>
> *In vain I have tried to kill myself twice. If I found in the depths of my weakness and my cowardice, however, the energy to disappear, if I finally succeed, you will never, ever tell Vally, will you, that it's for her that I am dying, and that she alone dealt me the final blow?*
>
> *The very pure amity of Ione was once my consolation and my refuge. Since her disappearance, I no longer have anything on earth.*

The fortnight that followed my first encounter with Vally was nothing but an ecstatic stupor, an enchanted splendor. Yes, during that time, I did not think, I lived. And yet I knew that she did not love me, that I was deceiving myself, as she was deceived. I knew that it was too late, and I took pleasure in the Irremediable.

It is not her fault if she could not love me. Nor is it mine. Do not blame her, since I do not blame her myself.

You are afraid of death, you, the poet of light, roses and Aphrodita. You, the belated of Lesbos, you fear death; for myself, I love it like a distant mistress. I am from the North, I love the mists that veil the mystery of real things; above all, I love the cool darkness.

I hate life. I do not know how or why I still exist.

Everything that I write is futile, weak, and impotent: as impotent as my thought, as weak as my heart, and as futile as my life. I rejoice in the memory of Ione's death. I am triumphant in the certainty of her repose. She is no longer suffering the oppression of existence, she is no longer anything but a perfume drifting in the depths of the night, a drop of sap in a blade of grass . . .

Dolor! Oh, the banality and the monotony of dolor! It is vulgar, since it belongs to everyone. It is the graceless prostitute that the crowd possesses. For having known it, there remains to me a lassitude mingled with disgust . . .

Vally! She has divine soulful smiles and un-expected tears. But above all she has implacable cruelties. I want to love her as one loves a dead woman. I only want to think any longer about the incomparable that is in her, of the feverish languor of our rare kisses, and the sadness of tender hours.

A portrait of her, which I had commissioned some time ago, has finally reached me, thanks to the complicity of an ironic Destiny. The raw wound of my being has been envenomed again by the contemplation of that face and those lips. Oh, those cold eyes, which have pierced my soul with their gaze devoid of tenderness!

She was my first amour, you see; I have only ever loved her. I believe that I shall never be able to love another woman with that same furious and wild passion.

I cannot forget her in the hours when I want to distract myself from that obsession. I have paid discreet court to a Spanish woman as fervently perfumed as a night in Mytilene. But that is only a game devoid of importance, a simple theme of conversation on which it is more agreeable to embroider than on the exces-sively worn theme of rain and fine weather. It resembles true love as the pain of a child re-sembles the agony of a martyr.

Doesn't it?

I dream of a death that would be a sensual-ity, a death that would be a consolation for life. And that death would be the impossible happi-

*ness that one has never glimpsed. The obsession
with that death is like a desire that is exalted
toward a beloved woman.*

San Giovanni addressed a gently mocking letter to me.
She unleashed a few sharp sarcasms at me and mocked
my inconstancy. She referred persistently to the Spaniard
with the eyes of the abyss.

I replied to her immediately:

> *Do you not know, friend, that psychology
> is mistaken almost as infallibly as medicine?
> You have fallen into the most profound error in
> believing that my love for Vally is conjugated
> in the past. Everything is finished between us;
> that is the best of reasons for me to continue to
> adore her.*
>
> *I committed a grave fault in exasperating
> her with my imbecile jealousy. But that jeal-
> ousy was very special. I did not criticize her at
> all when she knelt before feminine beauty, but
> my pride revolted at the thought of sharing her
> smiles, her promises and even her kisses with
> vulgar beings.*
>
> *As for the Sevillan brunette, O grossly
> abused seeress, I shall see her again tomorrow
> after a week's absence, and that thought is in-
> different to me. She has the perfidy of the Other,
> the Unique, without the charm and the magic
> of the entire being that once ensorcelled me.*
>
> *That does not prevent my new sovereign
> from being utterly exquisite. She has little intel-
> ligence, but a great deal of subtle cunning.*

Perhaps I am telling you all this lightly. The truth is that I am adrift in dolor. I hate Vally passionately. I would see her suffer with delight; and yet I would give my brain and my blood to spare her the slightest anguish. I can do no more. I love her.

Au revoir, poet of Mytilene, pious disciple of Psappha. Until when? I don't know. I can't envisage the future when the present has such a dolorous intensity. Perhaps you'll feel a little sorry for me, since you are as loyal a friend as you are subtle, and entirely delightful when you don't indulge in psychology.

I dare not kiss your hands, San Giovanni. You have hands that are almost virile, hands that possess, which grasp and hold, but never let go. I have, as you know, a passion for hands, which are more eloquent than faces.

I remember how Ione, for hours on end, contemplated her unhealthy hands with the dullness of old ivory . . .

Nor do I dare shake your hand as a comrade, for you have perverse hands, San Giovanni, and they disconcert me. Long, sinuous fingers make me too anxious. All things considered, I will quite simply bid you: Au revoir.

I left divine Toledo in order to plunge myself into the Moorish dream. The Alhambra was a pious enchantment for me. The *Sala de las Dos Hermanos* became dearer to me than all the rest. By a kind of sortilege of memory, I saw the two royal sisters Zorayda and Zorahayda.

They were sitting facing one another on either side of the fountain. The singing water was shining in the shadow, and their eyes were thoughtful as they contemplated it. The immutable reverie of the guzla players fell asleep less harmoniously. Sometimes, the princesses intoned a bizarre chant, and their voices dominated the music of the fountain.

Their gazes, simultaneously close and distant, sought one another through a cool mist. And every time their eyes summoned one another and confessed to one another thus, they shivered with a marvelous anguish . . .

But the fountain separated them from one another more efficaciously than all the doors of the palace. The fountain seemed to them to be an insurmountable obstacle. They smiled at one another palely through the mist of water. They never dared to sit down next to one another and hold hands. They never dared to unite their passionate and solitary lips. They died without destroying in their souls the infinite charm of desire and regret.

XVI
[Spring. Grieg.]

TOWARD the end of winter I tore myself away from the marvelous city and returned to Paris, with the cowardly hope of seeing again, for a moment, the fugitive beauty of Vally.

The sadness of spring was in me. The revolt of the young plants against imminent death, the futile effort of life, oppressed me like a suffering. What memories in the heart of renewals!

I was strolling around the lake, my eyes vaguely charmed by the reflections of trees on the surface, when a limpid voice made me shudder. It was a friend of San Giovanni, Dagmar, a young poet whom I had once admired for her delicate coloring of old Saxe. Her short curly hair haloed her with child-like grace, and her eyes, a puerile blue, opened wide, as if ecstasized by a tale of enchantment. She seemed the juvenile incarnation of May.

"How somber you are in this beautiful sunlight!" she said, her bright eyes smiling.

"The joy of others saddens my egotism, Dagmar."

She considered me with an astonished compassion.

"And Vally? A year ago you were her guard dog, meaning no offense."

"Oh, have no fear, I still have the cult of the absurd. I haven't forgotten Vally; it's Vally who has lost the memory of my modest existence."

"You must have suffered a great deal. You no longer have the same face. Though without wrinkles and white hair, you give an impression of decline and old age. I hesitated for a moment before recognizing you. I'm very good, fundamentally, in spite of my eccentric humor of a spoiled child. I'll listen to the tale of your woes, even if it's interminable. It's the best means of cure. By dint of talking about something, one end up becoming detached from it, for one wearies even of one's dearest dolors."

"Perhaps you're right, little April eglantine. But you're frightening me slightly; you resemble the morning too much."

"The morning is sometimes very mild, when it rises after a feverish night," she said. "It's necessary not to fear the morning. I've seen it wandering in the boscage, to see whether the red roses were open during the night. And with an infinitely compassionate gesture, it appeases the long insomnia of tobacco flowers, which finally go to sleep one by one."

"Sleep . . ." I murmured. "It's such a long time since I've enjoyed veritable slumber. I've learned to love in insomnias that bring me nocturnal thoughts so different from the thoughts of the day, and the very clear perception of Invisible Presences . . . Ione sometimes returns during the silence of midnights. Her Florentine dress, her dark red velvet dress seems a reflection of the setting sun in the depths of the darkness. She gazes at her pale hands . . . She had such beautiful and gentle hands, the hands of a sister and a consoler. But her eyes are always lowered, and she never murmurs a single word."

"Don't think about the dead. Let the dead bury their dead."

"It's because I'm closer to the dead than the living, Dagmar. How I love your name of a daughter of the North! A name more vigorous than the sea breeze; a fresh and joyful name, in your resemblance. The names of women are sometimes strangely evocative. Maries all have dolorous eyelids, like faded violets. The eyes of Sibyls are a mysterious vague blue and are lost in the beyond. Eleonores are kneaded from music and perfumes. They have profound hair in which datura petals are sprinkled. Elisabeths are strangely imperious; their gazes are as tenacious as memory. The smile of Lucies is as soft as starlight. It's necessary to fear Faustines, as perverse as witches and as cruel as Roman empresses. The soul of Blanches has the purity of expiatory lilies. Adelaides have the tragic lips of predestined lovers. Hélènes are as beautiful as statues."

"That's a verity that has not appeared to me."

She paused.

"I adore tales of enchantment. When I was little, my wooden horse lifted me up, a fabulous charger, toward the distances where the elves were playing in the moonlight. I've kept the soul of a child, astonished by the fantastic stories told on long winter evenings."

"You're charming, Dagmar. I'll come with you with great pleasure. For your sparkle, I'll abandon my solitude. If it's true that every person finds their image in the animal kingdom, you resemble a hummingbird."

"And what does Vally resemble?" the curious child asked, her eyes shining.

"A wild swan."

A heavy sadness circled my forehead, like a band of darkness.

"You're a very incomprehensible being," said the young poet, in order to deflect the course of my imagination. "How many people have you loved on earth?"

"I've loved in amity, and my very pure sister is dead. I've loved amorously, and that was a disaster. Today, Dagmar, I love solitude."

"Well, you'll forsake it for me. Come to see me tomorrow. You'll find Eva there, whom you've nicknamed the Goddess of the Sunset because of the red and brown gold of her hair."

"I remember her, in fact. She enchants me because, although luminously young, she nevertheless incarnates all the melancholies of Autumn. Her hair is like a glory around her pale face. She must have cherished, with a very dolorous tenderness, a past that she dares not remember."

"Well, no, you won't see her. You talk about her with too much fervor. I want to be the unique idol in my sanctuary."

I yielded to that ingenuous caprice, in which I found everything.

"Your desires are the solemn orders of Destiny, Child Divinity."

I went to see Dagmar the next day, a little less sad for having seen the freshness of her smile. She had put on a dress of slightly barbaric brightness. Like all young people, she liked things that were resplendent and sparkling. Around her neck, a row of large turquoises resembled the necklace of a savage girl.

"Look," she exclaimed, "the lilac is just flowering in the garden. Let's go see the tortoise, whose ancient wisdom is meditating amid the verdure. It's so attentive and so taciturn that it seems to be listening to the grass growing and the roots plunging into the ground. Sometimes, it seems harmonious . . ."

"And doubtless is," I confirmed. "Didn't Hermes form the first lyre with the shell of a tortoise? And didn't Psappha say: 'Come, divine tortoise, and become melodious beneath my fingers . . .' I have the greatest veneration for tortoises."

The sun gilded her childlike curls. She smiled at me, and a sudden wild tenderness burned in my soul for that creature of sap and dew. I desired her, like blue water in the dawn.

And the brutal desire to bite those lips naively offered for a kiss, to bruise that rosy eglantine flesh, became so strong that I took my leave of Dagmar abruptly.

She said to me, very simply: "Until tomorrow."

That evening, I spoke thus to my grave soul, which disapproved of me:

"Why recoil before the certainty of a joy and perhaps a consolation? Hope is the only light thread that can guide us through the bitter labyrinth—a tenuous thread, ready to break, but perhaps salvation. I could drink that blue water of the dawn. I could respire that bouquet of eglantines. I could see the dawn without terror and could sleep all night . . ."

At that moment, I received a letter from Vally:

> *What an unstable thing your heart is! I believed that you had finally glimpsed me, that we could follow our common path in security and confidence. Raise your eyes, see better, contemplate me as I am. This dismal blind-*

ness cannot be, should not be! I tell you that it's impossible. I repeat it to you, with tears in the eyes. Oh, fear drying them up, those tears, of rendering me incapable even of weeping for you. In truth, every individual has to be similar to the appearance our obstinacy forms of them. Fear rendering me one day as ugly as the image that you fashion of me. Fear, by virtue of not comprehending me, rendering me incomprehensible. Fear, by reproaching me for my cruelties, rendering me cruel, and by criticizing me for my indifference, petrifying me. A thought can do us so much harm, and what you think of me does me more harm than you imagine, and more than I know myself.

Can it be that everything is consummated? Can it be that the you that I imagined, everything that there was of the sincere and passionate in your being, will disappear?

Are you only going to seek banal amours in future, in order to forget the passion to which you have sacrificed your entire existence?

You only embrace in order to betray. For myself, I have never yet committed treason. By accusing me of all basenesses, do you think that you are raising yourself up? What do you hope to gain by trampling gods broken by your hands? Their mutilated grace will haunt you forever. Your fake happiness will never equal the disgust you have for yourself.

Oh, to have given you that weapon against me, your cowardly amour!

I went out, prey to all tempests. Blue irises, which I glimpsed in a shop window, evoked the fresh beauty of Dagmar. I sent them to her with these words:

All night long I waited feverishly for the approach of dawn. It finally came, as ugly and solemn as a nativity. It seemed obscurely fearful of the unknown life. But what did the sadness of the dawn matter to me? Did I not have the light of hope within me?

Fearful of seeing it vanish, I dared not reflect on that new and fragile tenderness. I dared not confess to myself the uncertain joy that was delighting me, in the fear of seeing it vanish. I dared not go to Dagmar's house, and it was not until the approach of sunset that I found the courage to knock on her door.

She was standing on the perron, her eyes hypnotized by the sumptuous sky.

"Look at those clouds!" she cried. "They're like three very pious and very powerful kings, who are bringing vases of gold and ciboria ornamented with precious stones in order to adorn altars."

"You are," I said, "a fay princess who sings while playing with her opal necklace. She loves her opals, which are reflections of the rainbow between her fingers. While waiting for the unknown prince, she goes to sleep every night to the sounds of an invisible harmony to which her laughing little sisters, the fays, cause to murmur all around her."

Dagmar, fingering her opals, stimulated their flames capriciously.

"Opals," she murmured. "Oh yes, I love them. I also like round turquoises and sapphires."

"The Hebrews name the sapphire *the most beautiful thing*," I replied. "They were marvelous artists. The epic poem of the Old Testament is unsurpassed by any other poem. The book of Job quivers with a tragic breath whose beauty stupefies, like a drama by Sophocles. I have the most profound admiration for the dolorous art of that race of exiles, which has been able to make the world its homeland. But above all, the Oriental silhouettes haunt me of Sarah, Rebecca, Rachel, Bathsheba and Tamar. The proud splendor of Sarah was such that Abraham represented her as his sister, for he did not want to risk his life by exposing himself to the jealousy that possession of such magnificence would inspire. Rebecca appears to us eternally mirrored in a legendary well. Rachel was so harmoniously splendid that, for having seen her trample the red lilies of the field underfoot, Jacob waited for her for seven years. By bathing naked on her terrace, Bathsheba gave rise to a desire for murder in the soul of David, who, in order to raise her up to his throne, had the importunate husband killed. I'm reminding you of these oriental idylls, little Dagmar, knowing that you like tales."

She smiled, the pretty smile of a perverse child.

"Little opal soul, you must have listened to innumerable confessions—confessions murmured on evenings like this one, whispered at twilight, or sobbed in the darkness."

"I've had a great many lovers, yes."

"Of both sexes, Dagmar; for I've heard you sing:

For I would dance to make you smile, and sing
Of those who with some sweet mad sin have played . . .
And low Love walks with delicate feet afraid
'Twixt maid and maid . . .

You must have collected that song from the passionate lips of a lover . . ."

"I like the love of women and that of men," she confessed. "I don't share the grim exclusivism of San Giovanni and all the women who, for the love of women, hate and scorn the love of men. But I prefer the incomparable tenderness of women to the rude vehemence of men more often than not."

I considered her.

"Pretty poem in porcelain, what words are fluid enough to tell you my gratitude? I can see again, for having encountered on my route the dream in Saxe that you are."

She was still smiling, without responding. For a long time I contemplated her parted lips, like a wild rose.

"Would you like," she said, "to take me to see the fireworks that are being displayed tonight? I adore the ambitious rockets, the showers of stars and the broken rainbows . . ."

"Little princess, the humblest of your courtiers awaits with docility your most futile orders."

She took my arm. The contact of that slender body intoxicated me. The consciousness of my strength increased in my own eyes. I felt proud of having softened a being who dominates and protects. I loved Dagmar, the insouciant and frail creature. I loved the seductive child in her. Her childish perversity was one charm more, a charm of anxiety and disquiet.

. . . A comet launched forth vertiginously toward the nocturnal abyss. It rose up recklessly as far as the most distant constellations. Dagmar's eyes followed it, astonished and delighted. The wide eyes of a child . . . Then there was a brief thunder, and a cascade of azure radiance.

"Oh," sighed Dagmar, "the snow of blue stars. Can you see them? Can you see them?"

She addressed me as *tu*, as a child with to a little comrade. She did not even know what she was saying, entirely given to the ecstasy of those shooting stars, green, white and red.

"How beautiful it is," she murmured, "that lightning before the stars. One moment, the whole sky is as white as the Milky Way! Now it's streaming with the heroic blood of giants . . . Oh, its decorated with crimson . . . it's like a vast carpet of violets . . . No, no, it's greener than the ocean on a spring evening. How beautiful it is, and how happy I am!"

Her eyelids fluttered, and her dazzled eyes sought mine in order to surprise the reflection of her joy there. I laughed like her, I laughed at her laughter. In truth, we had the light souls of two infants . . .

. . . But when the last rocket went out, my gaiety fell with it. We went back via an avenue of centenarian oaks.

"I'm almost afraid of these trees," said Dagmar, shivering. "They're higher than the vault of a Gothic cathedral. I'd be afraid, I'd be very afraid, if you weren't here . . ."

She huddled against me, with a chilly gesture. I would have liked to carry her far away, to lie her down on a bed as soft as a sick-bed, as narrow as a cradle, and burn her fragile bare feet with intolerable kisses.

"Aren't you tired, Dagmar?"

She looked at me with her eyes of a brazen page.

"A little."

The luminous laughter of her eyes belied her words. We sat down on a marble bench that the shadow covered, as thick and warm as moss.

As irresistible as an instinct, the desire to stroke that virginal flesh gripped me powerfully. I drew closer to her.

"Pretty, oh, too pretty, why have I so much anguish in loving you?"

She was not astonished, and not offended. She did not withdraw her hand, candidly white.

"I don't understand you . . . In fact, I've never been able to understand you. You're a bizarre and complex being . . ."

At that moment I sensed within me the primitive impulse of simian and cruel little boys, who amuse themselves by hurting and terrifying a wild dove. I would have liked to make that rosy Apriline face pale, for the wild joy of seeing the living intensity of an irresistible emotion in those eyes. To cause to vibrate, in that indifferent being, terror or amour—what did it matter? To cause a tremor, even of anger or disgust!

"Tell me again, and better, that you love me," commanded the imperious child.

"If I confessed the barbaric covetousness with which I love you, I might frighten you. Hatred is perhaps more intense and more durable than amour. It's as beautiful and as sacred as amour itself. The person who can't hate can't love. Among all poets, Dante moves me the most, because of the power of hatred that was in him, which was the equal of the power of his amour. Implacable enemies are also the most passionately tender lovers. Alighieri would have adored Beatrice less if he had hated his adversaries less. I love you with all the ardor of my antique hatreds, Dagmar."

"You have a frightful fashion of loving."

"O my lover of the dawn! If you knew, however, with what soft tenderness I surround you! It's simple, like everything that is profound. Prose perhaps expresses veritable ardor better than verse. My tenderness is very simple, but I would weave it in a thousand phrases, in order that it would appear eternally new to you. I want to render it versatile and changing, like the opals and the rainbows that you prefer . . ."

She inclined her forehead on my shoulder.

"I love you, Dagmar, with such an indulgent caress of the soul that your future treasons will never waken the slightest anger in me. And yet, if I loved you later with a passion like the one that ravaged me . . . who knows?"

The scarlet vision of the Past dazzled me with its bloody reflection. I sank into that terrible and dear contemplation . . .

XVII

[Morning. *Allegretto pastorale*. Grieg.]

AMONG all flowers, Dagmar preferred the unconscious lilacs of the renewal. Vally liked gardenias,
delicately artificial, which withered at the slightest touch.

"You're more eglantine than ever," I murmured. "I've
never seen freshness comparable to yours."

And the sudden thought came to me that it would be
unexpected and sweet to forget, next to that adolescence,
my long expiatory tortures. A laughter of perfumes, an
evocation of April, after the darkness of the abyss in
which my soul had been lost for such a long time. For
her it would be the caprice of an hour of ennui, and for
me, the unhoped-for consolation. It would be my heart
torn out of my breast and no longer torturing me with its
feverish beating.

But an anxiety retained me. Would I dare to put my
excessively heavy heart in the hands of a child?

Dagmar's laughing eyes were like spring water bathed
with blue daylight.

"What are you thinking about," she asked me. "Your
thoughts always make me anxious. You have such a somber gaze and such a bitter mouth. One would think them
the gaze and mouth of an old hermit, whose eyelids are

accustomed to darkness and whose taciturn lips have the crease of silence."

"I was thinking about Villiers de l'Isle Adam's Soeur Aloyse.[1] The eyes of the soul have never contemplated a more ideal face of an amorous virgin. I was also thinking that you resemble her, Dagmar, more joyful and less fervent, however."

I looked into the depths of her blue eyes at all the springtime that was reflected there.

"If you want to put your unsuspicious hand of a little girl in mine, Dagmar, I'll respire next to you the air of the dawn."

Her exceedingly clear eyes did not flinch under my gaze, somber with fear and desire. And, in her perverse candor, she extended her savant lips, her ingenuous lips, toward me.

"Have you no fear, Dagmar?"

My voice tore the invisible veils that the silence had just woven around us.

"Of what could I be afraid?"

"My love."

"Is it necessary to fear love?" she asked, so simply that I recoiled before the kiss that she was offering me. I recoiled as an individual that dementia has struck, taking a step back before the murder conceived in an insensate hour.

I took her frail hands in mine.

"Aren't you afraid of my hands, Dagmar? See how they've taken your hands, how they're compressing them, how they're possessing them."

She uttered the faint cry of a wounded skylark.

---

1 Soeur Aloyse is a character in Villiers de l'Isle Adam's unfinished but celebrated posthumously-published drama *Axël* (1890).

"You've crushed my fingers. You've hurt me . . ."

"And it's thus that they'll always hurt you, for they're violent hands, which have nearly become criminal hands. They might have tightened mortally around an exceedingly fragile neck, as fragile as your child-like neck. Vally once said to me that I have an evil soul, and that what I love most in amour is the anger and hatred. But there's still room in me for a pity that becomes tender before exquisite, confident weakness. You won't suffer from your puerile curiosity, Dagmar . . ."

XVIII
[Ballade, Op. 47, Part I. Chopin.]

THE maid with light curls went away for long days. I thought about her as one smiles at ancient childhoods . . .

Toward the end of a rainy afternoon, I was lingering in the library, which was blue with smoke and shadows, when the door opened. Dagmar advanced toward me, hesitantly.

"I've come to give you some very serious news," she said, in a vaguely hasty voice. "But first let me warm myself up and dry my soaking dress a little."

I lit a capricious fire for her. The flames made her excessively bright eyes shine.

"Give me a cigarette."

From her childishly greedy lips, a smoke was exhaled more subtle than an opium dream.

"I love the dusk as I would love a woman," I whispered, contemplating her.

"Dusk," she replied, "is like a woman weeping, a woman weeping alone in a silent room, where white flowers are wilting. The petals fall silently, one after another, and the moment is quivering with shameful dreams. In the distance, Memories in floating tunics pass by. Stars shine at their sandals . . ."

"You're a poet, like Eranna of Telos, the virgin of genius who died at nineteen and was loved by Psappha. But what's the grave news that you mentioned just now?"

She blushed faintly.

"You told me once that I was a little princess waiting on the terrace for the arrival of the Husband. My eyes, weary of the monotonous flat whiteness of the road, were searching the horizon in vain. I waited for long months on the terrace . . ."

She paused, and then, with a tremulous sigh, said: "The prince for whom I was waiting has come to me . . ."

There was an anguished silence.

A delicate Saxe shepherdess, who resembled Dagmar, was playing mute music on porcelain pies. Dolorously, I picked up the excessively pretty and excessively frail ornament, and I broke it.

Dagmar extended her imploring hands toward me.

"Spare me your rancor. I don't deserve it."

"I have no rancor in your regard, little princess."

"I tremble for my happiness," she said, shivering. "Society is like a dragon that never falls asleep, the cruel dragon of tales of enchantment. Oh, who will defend us against the hatred of the world? We're two children, he and I, lost in the dark forest."

Rain was falling, softer than attenuated music. The rain isolated our anxieties, like a drawn curtain. It separated us from the world and people. It made a noise like the silk of long trains.

"I don't know why," I said, in order to veil with speech the torment of my soul, "the rain reminds me of distant waves."

"Waves," murmured Dagmar, "and pebbles . . . I seem to see tides casting silver and glaucous flowers toward us."

"Dagmar," I sobbed, "divinely perverse and candid child, can it be that our routes are separating forever?"

"We've picked the pale roses of amity together," she replied.

Slowly, she stood up.

"My life is different from yours. I was cloistered behind a hawthorn hedge, and I scarcely divine the menacing ugliness of society. I don't know human existence. I don't know the passions and anguish reflected in your sore . . . your wicked . . . eyes . . ."

"In truth, Dagmar you haven't known human existence. That's why I haven't dared to love you."

She turned away, pensively.

"Adieu," she said, in a whisper.

"Adieu, Dagmar . . ."

As she went, she brushed the broken statuette with her Kate Greenaway dress with long pleats.

XIX
[Ballade. Op. 47, Part II. Chopin.]

DAGMAR had ventured into marriage like a child, confiding herself to a frail boat devoid of oars and a rudder, drifting toward the nocturnal Ocean.

Without a fortune, she had married a young man without a fortune. And yet, neither of them possessed the combative strength, nor the exact and practical vision of things that are the only protection against a mediocre life, even more terrible than poverty. Both of them adored ingenuous luxury naively, the fixed laughter of gems, the unfurling of landscapes and the multiple aspect of renewed joys.

Dagmar had accepted blindly the most redoubtable Unknown. She was not frightened before the mystery of Beings to come. Insouciant for them as for herself, she delivered the entire future to perfidious Hazard . . .

And the young husband, as irreflective as her, abandoned himself with an equal ignorant weakness to the caprice of an uncertain Destiny. They were, in truth, two children ingenuously dazzled by chimeras, lost in the dark forest.

On the day of their marriage, I was saddened for that barbarically immolated virginal grace. Hideous maternity would deform that asexual body, and conjugal rut would pollute that flesh kneaded of puerile eglantines . . .

I remained unconsolable before that shredding of a dream . . .

XX
[Nocturne Op. 48. Chopin.]

THE torment of April was finally extinct. The summer, dear to Our Lady of Fevers, surged forth from the burning earth. The image of Vally reigned implacably over the torrid hours. The image of Vally consumed my blood and desiccated my marrow. I dreaded flowers, as sly adversaries; I dreaded music, as a perfidious enemy; for flowers and music concealed all the treasons of memory. They evoked, in a cowardly fashion, the cruel blue eyes that I hated and adored simultaneously. The voluptuous angers of old were tearing me apart, like as many charming monsters. Words vibrated in my memory. Sometimes, teeth clenched for a mute defense, I struggled against the force that drew me toward Her . . .

I avoided my Loreley's friends, and yet I hoped for a circumstance as unexpected as it was mutedly desired, a superior order of destiny that would force me to see her again, or at least to hear mention of her. Events served me. I learned that Vally's secret engagement had become an official engagement.

I had the cowardice to write to her. My letter went unanswered. I knew the inexpressible anguish of those walled up and buried alive. I even lost the strength to weep for myself, the unique and tender consolation of the afflicted.

One day, however, I awoke with a less heavy soul. It seemed to me that perfumes of violets had bathed my forehead while I slept.

I no longer had the oppression that stifled me when I awoke. I no longer feared the sunlight coming in through the open window or the perfume of honeysuckle that rose from the garden.

I asked myself very quietly what unknown sweetness had thus dissipated the pestilential breath of Our Lady of Fevers. And, looking outside, I perceived that summer had just fled before the autumn.

The appeasement of faded flowers infiltrated into me. I wandered by the water into which the russet tresses of willows were dipping. I contemplated the chrysanthemums whose saddened hues harmonized with the withered foliage. Trees, more beautiful for being bare, were twisting their delicate winter skeletons.

The consolation of autumn rendered the world less intolerable. I had an agonizing soul, which rejoiced in dying. With an uncertain expectation, I raised my eyes. And in front of me, serene in the serenity of October, I perceived Eva.

She seemed the very incarnation of autumn. In her long hands, of martyrs, chrysanthemums were expiring, mingled with dead leaves. The melancholy pleats of her dress fell around her. She was mounted in stained glass windows more splendid than the rainbow and the sunset . . .

I dreamed that once, in an excessively noisy city, where I had had a soul dolorously wounded by the noise, I had murmured her mystical name, her saint's name. And suddenly, the ringing of aerial bells floated above the tumult of the discordant streets. The pious carillon sang her name, proclaimed it, cast it to the winds:

"Eva! Eva! Eva!"

She came toward me. No vain speech broke the charm of the mystery. I understood her, and she understood me similarly.

"My sweet Autumn, my dear Autumn," I stammered, finally.

I thought that she and I were standing on the threshold of eternity. Invisible stained glass threw a glory so miraculous around her that I could not sustain its glare. A hope as vast as the sadness rose up in my heart.

She only replied to me with her grave smile.

I don't know why the image of Dagmar, that poem in porcelain, loomed up between us with its disquieting charm of fragility.

An anguish more terrible than any human anguish gripped me at that moment. My eyes were attached to Eva's eyes, distant and gray, as if seen through clouds of incense.

I repeated the words of yesterday: "Aren't you afraid, Eva?"

"I fear nothing," she said.

It was like a murmur on an organ in the depths of crepuscular chapels.

"Will you be stronger than my sickness?" I implored.

"I shall be stronger than all human woes, since I am pity."

There was a religious silence around us. I dared not sob to her: "I love you!"

XXI
[Scherzo of Sonata Op. 35. Chopin.]

A year later, the summer evening, white with clematis, brought us together in the library with old English furniture. Everything in Eva's house, where I had found a refuge, was cordial and simple. Things were welcoming there, with a sincere bounty. The walls, coated with thick and somber paper with a velvet softness, protected confidential conversations perpetually. The armchairs were propitious to meditation. The atmosphere of peace and security enveloped one as soon as the threshold was crossed. One respired a charming odor of faded flowers and old wood. On the mantelpiece, next to the portrait of Ione, white violets were leaning.

"I have another surprise to announce to you," Eva said to me, in a very quiet voice, as if meditative. "That old Norman clock that you installed in the dining room has acclimated so well amid the Queen Anne furniture that I heard it pronounce quite distinctly just now:

"*One, two, three, four, five, six, seven, eight.*"

"It has learned English very quickly, hasn't it?"

"Furniture has obscure sympathies and antipathies," I corroborated. "One of my friends assures me that she has a chair in her house hostile to any usurper. It would be impossible for anyone but her to remain in it for more than ten minutes. The muted inimity that emanates from it repels unconsciously."

"Perhaps it's true. What saddens me slightly is that these items of furniture, which we've loved, and which are impregnated with us slightly, depend on us, and will fall into other hands, which will possess them as entirely as we have possessed them."

She fell silent and, in spite of the melancholy of her words, a happy silence reigned between us.

Suddenly, Eva's lips creased in a slight contraction.

"It seems to me that I can see, saddening the depths of your gaze, the shadow of Vally," she said, anxiously.

Her voice quivered with anguish slightly as it pronounced the name of my Past. In spite of the confident mildness with which my soul was impregnated, I paled at that invocation. My eyes looking into Eva's, I replied to her thought.

"I've found peace, Eva, but I haven't yet found forgetfulness. When one has loved someone as I loved that woman, it can never become indifferent. One can never abolish in oneself the Past that caused incomparable suffering."

"You're right," Eva sighed, deeply.

She hesitated, and then went on:

"The moment is very grave. From the unknown, a kind of presentiment is entering, through the open window . . ."

Suddenly, I respired a strange perfume, more subtle than the perfume of flowers, which was exhaled from the garden, and rose toward me. I shuddered, as if before an indeterminate peril.

"I'll reveal to you now, *since it's necessary*, what I've hidden from you until now, fearing for the health of your sick soul. Vally's engagement with the Prostitute has been definitively broken. The Prostitute has finally sold himself for a dowry even more tempting than Vally's . . ."

Eva stopped, her eyelids divinely thoughtful, before murmuring very slowly: "Vally has returned . . ."

She waited. I understood the immense significance of those few simple words. Vally had wearied of the infamous comedy. She had become herself again, the Princess of Neglected Altars, the one before whom my soul had once knelt. The infamy of that man was not interposed between us. I could take back my Loreley. I could go to her, begging her to forgive me for all the harm she had done me and I had done to myself for her. I could revive the ardent sufferings and hateful sensualities, of which I retained the cruel imprint incurably.

At that evocation, it seemed to me that I was reborn in the flame that had once consumed my dolorous flesh. That flame sprang forth around me, magnificently frightful, and I quivered with all the exaltation of a triumphant death. I regretted the past bitterness even more than the acute and brief joys.

"Vally," I stammered. "Vally . . ."

The dazzlement disappeared, and my eyes encountered once again the mystically clouded eyes of Eva. They had the sadness that is dormant in the eyes of Saints impotent to soothe the dolors kneeling before them.

"The mirage has dissipated, Eva."

She stood up, diaphanous in the semi-darkness.

"I'll leave you to your two former councilors, silence and solitude."

"Are you not my silence, Eva? Are you not my solitude?"

Slowly, and with infinite gentleness, she disengaged her hands from mine, which were trying to hold her back.

"No. Your solitary soul must decide a destiny which concerns no one else. Solitude is the natural fate of the Individual, who is born alone, who suffers alone and who dies alone. No compassion, no matter how burning and full of pity it is, can infringe the sacred Law."

She disappeared into the depths of the dusk, which enveloped her like a veil . . .

I lingered, dreaming obscurely. The vision of Eva put into the imprecise light a supernatural reflection of stained glass . . .

Gradually, the darkness was illuminated by an equivocal smile. It was Vally, the flower of Selene, the Undine and the Loreley. She incarnated eternal feminine Temptation. A cruel ambiguity sharpened the steely gleam of her gaze. I thought that those two women were the two archangels of the Best and the Worst: Vally, the Perverse Archangel; Eva, the Redemptive Archangel . . . Vally, the glow of the greening moon, Vally, perfumed with poisons, adorned with aconite and belladonna; Eva, bearing on her forehead the red aureole of a martyr, Eva, shredding expiatory lilies under her footsteps . . .

I pronounced aloud, invoking I know not what invisible Presences: "Choose . . ."

"Never choose," interjected a contralto voice, an androgynous voice whose familiar tone responded to my hesitation. "One always regrets what one has not chosen."

"My sweet San Giovanni, what would you advise me to do in this indecisive hour?"

"I advise you to return to Vally."

"I don't recognize your habitual wisdom there."

She smiled strangely; as the evening smiled at its image reflected in the water.

"No word of wisdom is worth as much as the laughter of folly," she affirmed. "I believe, or, rather, I am certain that, if you threw yourself at her knees, as before, Vally would not refuse you her pardon."

"It's too late, San Giovanni. Irreparable words have been pronounced. Between her and me, henceforth, there is the image of another woman."

Her gesture of impatience astonished me dolorously.

"I have always preferred violence to tenderness and passion to amour," she said emphatically, in her imperious tone. "That is why I criticize your cowardice in having esteemed happiness more highly than radiant suffering."

"I'm neither a salamander nor a phoenix, San Giovanni, and I can't live in that which destroys and consumes."

"So much the worse for you; you'll never be a poet. No poet has ever been happy. I don't say that for myself," she went on, with some sadness. "I've never arrogated that sacred title, to which I have no veritable right. No one is, in any case, a poet or a saint while alive. But you won't be a poet in death, since you haven't been able to love."

"I've loved to the limit of my strength," I said, defending myself. "No one has the right to ask any more of a human being. Ibsen's terrible *All or Nothing* I've accepted joyfully . . . Later, I was exhausted and I renounced the vain struggle. Like Dante, I've wandered in the stormy night, and I've knocked on the door of the monastery, imploring peace . . . A Nun opened up to me the sanctuary in which my soul was divinely consoled."

San Giovanni was only listening to me distractedly.

"Dagmar was coming back from the traditional and imbecile honeymoon voyage when I encountered her," she said. "She asked me whether you harbored a slight resentment against her. Why hold it against her that she was unable to cure you by loving you with the terrible ardor that you demanded of her?"

"I've never harbored resentment against any woman, no matter how great the harm is that she did me or wanted to do me. The injustices of women and their angers are like the injustices and angers of the Gods. It is necessary to accept them with love and submit to them with resignation. And certainly, no individual is culpable for not loving another. That's why Vally has never committed the slightest sin in my regard."

San Giovanni considered me, her gaze softened.

"Listen to the counsel of music," she said. "Listen to the counsel of flowers. The only oracles that remain to us from marvelous Antiquity are songs and perfumes. Music will bring you back to your Pagan Priestess by virtue of the magic of dream. Flowers will bring you back to your Loreley by means of the prestige of memory . . ."

She lifted the crimson door-curtain, and I heard the frisson of her dress draw away gradually . . .

I remained in my troubled solitude. Stars were singing in the profundity of space.

Eva, very pale, came in without a word and handed me a piece of paper. Then she quit me, in a stir of dead leaves.

Thanks to the semi-darkness, I read:

I am waiting in the garden.

The strange perfume, more imperious than ever, attracted me like a vehement appeal. I stood up and frayed a passage for myself through the nocturnal foliage.

XXII
[Nocturnes. Chopin.]

WITH an odor of slumber the tobacco flowers calmed the violet air. Their perfidiously languorous breath dispensed maleficent dreams.

The silence was terrible by virtue of its intensity. There was an anguished silence that enfevered the night. The plants were vaguely fearful of the words that we were about to pronounce, and the trees were thoughtful, like grave prophets saddened by the future . . .

Vally, her hair more fluidly green and her eyes bluer than the moon, was waiting. Her imprecise silhouette stood out against the blue-tinted grass, framed by the glaucous foliage. Momentarily, I contemplated the form and visage of my Past.

"Vally . . ."

She did not raise her eyes. She was like the statue of a dead woman.

"Vally . . ."

Finally, the immobile pallor of that apparition became animated.

"I've come to you to take you back. You belong to me, for I am your first love. You belong to me, above all, because I was the first to make you suffer. You cannot annihilate the past that links us indissolubly. I am your Destiny. You can flee me, but you can never forget me."

"I shall never forget you, Vally. I would never want to forget you. You will never be a stranger to me, or indifferent."

A victorious gleam traversed Vally's lunar eyes. I divined her thought of barbaric triumph. The pride of the conqueror masculinized her despotic voice.

"I knew that, and that's why I've come to you."

As before, I feared her cruel smile.

"I won't go with you, Vally."

She looked at me fixedly. The crease of her lips contracted with an inexpressible scorn.

"I scarcely understood you, Vally, and I loved you poorly. I wasn't able to tame my jealous soul. I wasn't able to vanquish the rancor and the suspicions and the hatred that intensified and corrupted my miserable passion. I have been the most basely suspicious and bitter individual whoever rendered herself odious to herself. I have importuned you by torturing myself with a thousand refined tortures. I have been the executioner of my soul. For everything that was not worthy of you and of me, I beg your pardon in an infinite kneeling."

The disdainful eyes did not quit mine.

"You haven't been able to conquer me," Vally pronounced, slowly. "You had neither the strength, nor the patience, nor the courage to vanquish my hostile withdrawal from any individual who wants to dominate me."

"I'm not unaware of that, Vally. I'm not formulating the slightest reproach, the slightest complaint. I retain an inexpressible gratitude to you for having inspired in me the amour that I wasn't able to make you share."

"I said to you once: 'Only love me just enough to illuminate my existence.'"

"And I wasn't wise enough to obey you."

She was carrying, in a fold of her dress, orchids as avid as unassuaged lips. She detached them and shredded them one by one with her long, implacable fingers.

"I never let you believe that I would love you as you have loved me. You saw me from the first day as I was," she said. "I hoped to vanquish my indifference for you, but I wasn't able to triumph over my coldness in your regard. And yet, I would have liked so much to love you! It is necessary to feel sorry for me for being incapable of a unique and sincere passion, for I know nothing sadder in the world than wandering perpetually, wandering in quest of an inaccessible tenderness!

Eros has made me love without closing my eyes.

"You have done me an inexpiable wrong. You have not been able to console in me the Lover, the creature of cunning and cruelty, the creature of flesh who nevertheless wants the Impossible. The Impossible has not been accorded to her, so she has killed herself with anger and shame and everything. She is dead today."

"You're right," I sighed.

"If less terrible amours do not make more of you than you have been—which is to say, the being of all sacrifices and all absurd devotions—if less lacerating amours are bound to bring you down to their own level, if less willful individuals bend you to their fashion of being and living, send an appeal to me. I will come like a bird of prey and I will seize you in my iron claws, which will perhaps bruise you, but which will carry you away to infinite altitudes, toward aeries that those lovers of days and nights, with their mildness and their petty plaints, will never be able to attain or elevate you."

She had never spoken to me in the voice of melancholy and regret. I retreated into the shadow.

"Vally . . . Vally . . ."

"I will be quite different and better, oh, you'll see! Already, I've changed a little . . . at least, I believe so. I'm only afraid of terrible slumbers. I'm only afraid of mortal forgetfulness. Death is less frightful than Metamorphosis . . ."

"And yet, you've changed yourself, you say . . ."

"I have more need of you than I would have believed, and differently. I have need of you . . ."

The tobacco flowers were paling in the shadow. Their breath put my reason and my conscience to sleep. Their nocturnal perfumes were so powerful that they triumphed over everything that was not as subtle, perilous and perfidious as themselves.

E dell'antico amore sentii la gran Potenza . . .[1]

O perverse Beatrice, clad in living flame, O vision sprung from a cloud of flowers! O imperishably dolorous memory!

"One belongs to one's past," Vally emphasized. "Everything down here would be too facile if one could escape the consequences of one's actions. I am your Past and you belong to me."

1 This version of the line from the *Purgatorio* differs slightly from the version quoted in the 1905 novel.

"One belongs to one's future. I belong to my future . . . and to Eva."

"The Past is truer than the Future. The future is uncertainty, the Past is what is written in ineffaceable letters."

Vally's voice was sovereignly imposing. I replied to her with an evasive remark.

"I said to Eva this very evening: *I would like to spread throughout the universe a little of the joy that comes to me from your presence.*"

"What joy can equal dolor? Dolor is stronger than joy. One can forget a joy, one never forgets a dolor. I am your suffering, that is why you will never cease to love me. Suffering alone is true, and happiness is not."

"Why would the possible be ungraspable?" I asked. "I have the certainty that happiness is tangible, that it is as true as the dream. But it is necessary to struggle even more bitterly to keep it than to conquer it."

"I covet a higher ideal for you than happiness. I want you to be free, in order that nothing diminishes you by absorbing you. I want you to be free, in order that you can contemplate what is above you. You are so weak when you love, even if only slightly and confusedly, as you loved me. And I fear for us the harm that they will do you."

I listened with troubled astonishment to that new gravity in her voice.

"I am thinking," she said, "of the Passage of the Giant. The future is similar to a mountain road that it is necessary to hollow out in the rock. The crowd stops, hesitant and stupid, before the insurmountable blocks that overhang the gulf. But a giant lifts them up and marches on. He frays a heroic passage through the brambles and the stone. Thirst consumes him and solitude enfevers him.

He perishes before reaching the Other Slope. Then the irresistible force of all those weaknesses runs along the road that he has traced. They are seen to swarm in millions where the precursor giant died. If there is truly something great in you, do as he did; go toward your destiny. Scorn cowardly happiness; choose the better part, which is that of tears."

"I don't know whether happiness, infinitely rare, is inferior to suffering, the universal lot," I protested.

"Let's be calm and limpid, shall we? Let's not plunge thus into the depths of verity and lies. The night seems weary to me—just as weary as me. But tomorrow, I shall be reborn with the dawn, and I will be April for you, with indecisive laughter, April, whose joy conceals promises of sad harvests, crops still dormant."

"There can be no dawn in the past, Vally. The past dies with the last stars. Only the future is the dawn."

"I'm sickened by reason and verity. I'm sickened by everything that is not simple amour."

I replied with all my former sadness:

"Amour also has its hopeful dawns, its fervent middays, its melancholy sunsets and its long moonless nights. You know that better than I do, you who fear Metamorphosis more than Death."

Vally turned away, obliquely.

"Temptation only ever attracts the sated, and because your soul is sated with disgust, I know that you will come back to me. You will come back to me because disgust and lassitude only ever see one side of things. Nothing is good or bad in itself; that rule also applies to humans. You cannot judge me as clearly as I judge myself, but you say that you loved me and love me still. The pride with which you are obstinate in only considering my ugliness proves that there is within you a vampire intoxicated by ferocity. Personally, I am more fortunate, I see exclusively what I want to see, and then, little enough and poorly enough to safeguard my illusions.

"You will come back to me. I said this to you once: it is you who are the cruel one, since you make me suffer stupidly, and you do not place me, in a definitive fashion, in shelter from all suspicion. I play with men because I take pleasure in making them suffer, and because that amuses me sometimes. But I have never loved a man, that I can swear to you in all honesty.

"I also said to you: *Don't overwhelm me with jealousy and mistrust when I hold out my avid arms toward you and always want from you nothing but your tenderness. Do not destroy something beautiful in its invincible strength. I cling to you above passions and the days—all the rest is only a matter of ennui or nerves, and has no importance or duration.*"

"And an hour later, Vally, you expelled me from your presence with harsh words: *I don't love you . . . you exasperate me . . . you are the shadow on my road of lilies and moonlight.*"

"What have you done with your pale April?" sighed Vally. "I have in my soul an entire heritage of spring. Open your arms and your heart to me again. I won't reawaken any anguish in you. I won't bring you any vestige of a past that isn't ours. Piously, like those who enter a temple, I shall enter your heart, and if I find a joy there that is fading by virtue of already being old, I'll replace it with a freshly blossomed joy. I have a soul full of flowers when I think of the great Possible that contains all hopes . . ."

"I can't give you happiness, Vally. You're inclining toward me because I'm escaping you as a danger, because I'm fleeing you as a peril. I loved you too much not to fear you eternally. I've lost hope and confidence since . . . since you! But a Savior has come to me, an unhoped-for Savior . . . Eva . . ."

"You're stubborn in only seeing ugly and sad things in our past. Remember the lilies!"

The sky was like a marvelous ceiling of cedar, nacre and ivory. The trees were as svelte and white as Moorish columns. The night seemed a palace of Boabdil, meditating in all the dream of the Past.

"I remember, Vally."

"You've stolen a happiness to which you don't have any right. Remember your own words: *Amour is renunciation and sacrifice. Amour is a kneeling.*"

She stopped and said, liturgically:

"*Amour is a Calvary where roses flourish.*"

A dead serpent lay at our feet. An oblique ray of moonlight made the tarnished gold of its green scales glitter strangely, which seemed to quiver with a slow undulation. And I remembered the enigmatic phrases of San Giovanni:

> *Dead Serpents revive under the gaze of those who love them. The magical eyes of Liliths reanimate them, as moonlight reanimates stagnant waters . . . Dead Serpents insinuate themselves through the semi-darkness, where their eyes dart cruel gleams. For, being faithful, they serve the Liliths and lie in wait for the prey that they have designated to them.*

"What joy and what peace can ever equal the divine suffering that you once learned on my lips?" Vally demanded.

. . . Our Lady of Fevers was corrupting the garden with her mortal breath. The foxgloves and the belladonnas extended their perfumes and their poisons toward her. The reptiles crawled all the way to her paludal reliquary and brought her as an offering their venomous souls. A lunar leprosy corroded the trees, and the red roses bled like livid wounds. I wanted to flee the pestiferous garden, but I could not take my eyes off Vally's, and the hair greener and the eyes bluer than nocturnal gleams.

"Remember the lilies," she said, insistently.

A distant lamp cast a faint glow over the violent shadow in which the tobacco flowers were dying. That glow was coming from the bedroom of my Savior. That glow was as consoling as the calm reflection of starlight.

Then it disappeared . . . The darkness listened to the counsel of the dead Serpents. Vally's blonde morbidity attenuated further under the moonlight.

"A dolor sharper than joy, a joy more profound than dolor," she emphasized. "An amour more terrible than hatred, a hatred more voluptuous than amour . . . All the passion that scorns peace . . ."

Again the lamp cast a starry radiance. It was vacillating in Eva's hands; she was approaching us, pale and transparent . . .

In truth, those two women were like the archangels of Destiny: Vally, clad in green, Eva, clad in violet, both strangely luminous . . .

"This is the Hour of the Soul," Eva murmured.

Between the three of us, there was an anguished pause. What I was about to say was decisive and fatal. All of my indefinite existence depended on that momentary resolution. All the terror of the choice weighed upon me.

. . . When the final word was pronounced, a sigh rose from the penumbra.

"Adieu . . . and *au revoir* . . ."

A PARTIAL LIST OF SNUGGLY BOOKS

G. ALBERT AURIER *Elsewhere and Other Stories*

CHARLES BARBARA *My Lunatic Asylum*

S. HENRY BERTHOUD *Misanthropic Tales*

LÉON BLOY *The Desperate Man*

LÉON BLOY *The Tarantulas' Parlor and Other Unkind Tales*

ÉLÉMIR BOURGES *The Twilight of the Gods*

CYRIEL BUYSSE *The Aunts*

JAMES CHAMPAGNE *Harlem Smoke*

FÉLICIEN CHAMPSAUR *The Latin Orgy*

FÉLICIEN CHAMPSAUR
    The Emerald Princess and Other Decadent Fantasies

BRENDAN CONNELL *Unofficial History of Pi Wei*

BRENDAN CONNELL *The Metapheromenoi*

RAFAELA CONTRERAS *The Turquoise Ring and Other Stories*

ADOLFO COUVE *When I Think of My Missing Head*

QUENTIN S. CRISP *Aiaigasa*

LADY DILKE *The Outcast Spirit and Other Stories*

CATHERINE DOUSTEYSSIER-KHOZE *The Beauty of the Death Cap*

ÉDOUARD DUJARDIN *Hauntings*

BERIT ELLINGSEN *Now We Can See the Moon*

ERCKMANN-CHATRIAN *A Malediction*

ALPHONSE ESQUIROS *The Enchanted Castle*

ENRIQUE GÓMEZ CARRILLO *Sentimental Stories*

EDMOND AND JULES DE GONCOURT *Manette Salomon*

REMY DE GOURMONT *From a Faraway Land*

REMY DE GOURMONT *Morose Vignettes*

GUIDO GOZZANO *Alcina and Other Stories*

GUSTAVE GUICHES *The Modesty of Sodom*

EDWARD HERON-ALLEN *The Complete Shorter Fiction*

EDWARD HERON-ALLEN *Three Ghost-Written Novels*

RHYS HUGHES *Cloud Farming in Wales*

J.-K. HUYSMANS *The Crowds of Lourdes*

J.-K. HUYSMANS *Knapsacks*

COLIN INSOLE *Valerie and Other Stories*

JUSTIN ISIS *Pleasant Tales II*

MARCEL SCHWOB *The Assassins and Other Stories*

MARCEL SCHWOB *Double Heart*

CHRISTIAN HEINRICH SPIESS *The Dwarf of Westerbourg*

BRIAN STABLEFORD (editor)
Decadence and Symbolism: A Showcase Anthology

BRIAN STABLEFORD (editor) *The Snuggly Satyricon*

BRIAN STABLEFORD (editor) *The Snuggly Satanicon*

BRIAN STABLEFORD *The Insubstantial Pageant*

BRIAN STABLEFORD *Spirits of the Vasty Deep*

BRIAN STABLEFORD *The Truths of Darkness*

COUNT ERIC STENBOCK *Love, Sleep & Dreams*

COUNT ERIC STENBOCK *Myrtle, Rue & Cypress*

COUNT ERIC STENBOCK *The Shadow of Death*

COUNT ERIC STENBOCK *Studies of Death*

MONTAGUE SUMMERS *The Bride of Christ and Other Fictions*

MONTAGUE SUMMERS *Six Ghost Stories*

GILBERT-AUGUSTIN THIERRY *The Blonde Tress and The Mask*

GILBERT-AUGUSTIN THIERRY *Reincarnation and Redemption*

DOUGLAS THOMPSON *The Fallen West*

TOADHOUSE *Gone Fishing with Samy Rosenstock*

TOADHOUSE *Living and Dying in a Mind Field*

TOADHOUSE *What Makes the Wave Break?*

LÉO TRÉZENIK *Decadent Prose Pieces*

RUGGERO VASARI *Raun*

JANE DE LA VAUDÈRE *The Demi-Sexes and The Androgynes*

JANE DE LA VAUDÈRE *The Double Star and Other Occult Fantasies*

JANE DE LA VAUDÈRE *The Mystery of Kama and Brahma's Courtesans*

JANE DE LA VAUDÈRE *Three Flowers and The King of Siam's Amazon*

JANE DE LA VAUDÈRE *The Witch of Ecbatana and The Virgin of Israel*

AUGUSTE VILLIERS DE L'ISLE-ADAM *Isis*

RENÉE VIVIEN AND HÉLÈNE DE ZUYLEN DE NYEVELT
Faustina and Other Stories

RENÉE VIVIEN *Lilith's Legacy*

TERESA WILMS MONTT *In the Stillness of Marble*

TERESA WILMS MONTT *Sentimental Doubts*

KAREL VAN DE WOESTIJNE *The Dying Peasant*

www.ingramcontent.com/pod-product-compliance
Lightning Source LLC
Chambersburg PA
CBHW050238110726
47898CB00007B/2192